RAILROAD OF COURAGE

May you find
courage when
courage is needed —

Nny and

DAN/

Railroad
of Courage

Dan Rubenstein &
Nancy Dyson

RONSDALE PRESS

RAILROAD OF COURAGE
Copyright © 2017 Dan Rubenstein & Nancy Dyson

RONSDALE PRESS
3350 West 21st Avenue, Vancouver, B.C., Canada V6S 1G7
www.ronsdalepress.com

Typesetting: Julie Cochrane, in Minion 12 pt on 16
Cover Art & Design: Nancy de Brouwer, Massive Graphic Design
Paper: 55 lb. Enviro Book Antique Natural (FSC) 100% post-consumer
    waste, totally chlorine-free and acid-free

Ronsdale Press wishes to thank the following for their support of its publishing program: the Canada Council for the Arts, the Government of Canada, the British Columbia Arts Council, and the Province of British Columbia through the British Columbia Book Publishing Tax Credit program.

Canada Council   Conseil des arts
for the Arts   du Canada

Canada

BRITISH COLUMBIA
ARTS COUNCIL
An agency of the Province of British Columbia

Library and Archives Canada Cataloguing in Publication

Rubenstein, Daniel Blake, author
    Railroad of courage / Dan Rubenstein & Nancy Dyson.

Issued in print and electronic formats.
ISBN 978-1-55380-514-4 (softcover)
ISBN 978-1-55380-515-1 (ebook) / ISBN 978-1-55380-516-8 (pdf)

    1. Underground Railroad—Juvenile fiction. 2. Slaves—Juvenile fiction.
I. Rubenstein, Nancy, author II. Title.

PS8635.U2953R35 2017   jC813'.6   C2017-903887-7   C2017-903888-5

At Ronsdale Press we are committed to protecting the environment. To this end we are working with Canopy and printers to phase out our use of paper produced from ancient forests. This book is one step towards that goal.

Printed in Canada by Marquis Printing, Quebec

*This book is dedicated
to those individuals, black and white,
who formed the Underground Railroad,
a work of moral imagination driven
by the courage of the runaways*

CHAPTER ONE

Deciding

❧

MY NAME IS REBECCA and I was born into slavery in the spring of 1842 on a cotton plantation near Rock Hill, South Carolina. When I was twelve years old, I ran away with my ma Deborah and my pa Obadiah. The owner of the plantation, Grower Brown, was a hard man and all of us slaves were afraid of him. I worked in the kitchen while my pa and my ma worked in the fields. I have since travelled far from that life.

Grower Brown had a son named Master Jeff who was just as mean as his father, but his daughter, Miss Clarissa, was kind to me. Miss Clarissa and I, we were the same age so when Miss Clarissa's ma died giving birth to her, my ma was brought into the house to nurse her. We were like sisters but she was free and I was not.

As we grew up, we had to be careful around Miss Clarissa's father and brother. When they saw us playing together, they threatened to whip me and send me into the fields to work. Working the cotton was a hard job, and I was not very strong. Once, when Grower Brown said he would whip me, Miss Clarissa stood in front of me and told her father he would have to whip her, too. Grower Brown stared at his daughter, then cursed and sent me to work in the fields for the rest of the day. But he didn't whip me, thanks to Miss Clarissa, and the next day I was back working in the kitchen.

Grower Brown and Master Jeff both had terrible tempers, and they were cruel to the other slaves. Miss Clarissa told me that she would never let them hurt me, no matter how much they threatened, and I believed her, but I wondered whether she was strong enough to stand up to them. Miss Clarissa was my friend and I miss her. I hope someday we will be friends again, in a different world.

One day Grower Brown called a meeting of all the plantation owners in the county. I passed food and drink to the men gathered on the veranda. As they drank whiskey and ate fried chicken, they talked about the problem of runaway slaves. Every few weeks, slaves ran away from Grower Brown's plantation and other plantations. Most of them were caught. The others disappeared and we never knew what happened to them. My pa said it was foolish to run away, foolish and dangerous.

Master Jeff stood on a chair and spoke in a loud voice, "My father and I have called you here because we have a problem. Every month we lose slaves from our plantations. When those runaways reach northern towns, they walk the streets and act as if they are free men. But they are not free men; they belong to us. They're our property, just like our pigs and horses. The Founding Fathers of the United States of America protected our right to own slaves. North of the Mason–Dixon Line, the federal marshals should be arresting runaways and returning them to us. That's the law. But we know that the marshals are not catching them. What's worse is that some white people in the free states of the North take runaways into their homes, feed them, hide them and smuggle them into Canada. The law says those abolitionists should be fined, but the federal government does nothing so we've got to do something!"

Grower Brown looked proudly at his son as the

growers raised their glasses and shouted, "Amen, Jeff. Amen." Standing on that chair, Master Jeff stood taller than all the other growers, but Miss Clarissa stood in a corner, looking ashamed of her father and brother. She looked down at the floor as I moved among the growers, passing the fried chicken, filling their glasses with whiskey.

Master Jeff nodded to his father and continued, "Our runaway slaves are not being arrested because the abolitionists, those slave lovers, are pressuring the government to ignore the Fugitive Slave Act. But there is an answer—the Knights of the Golden Circle. Only the Knights are defending our right to own slaves, not only in the South but in Border States like Illinois and Ohio. They need our help; they need our money. They plan to form a secret army in the North, and when that army is organized, it will return our runaway slaves to us. To support that army, I ask you to join my father and me in forming a castle, a local branch of the Knights, right here in our county."

For the second time, the growers cheered Master Jeff's speech. They slapped him on the back and shouted, "You're right, Jeff. We own our slaves and runaways should be returned to us." They threw money into a big wide-brimmed hat that Master Jeff passed from man to man. They asked Master Jeff to be the leader of the castle and he was quick to agree. He promised them that he would go to Cincinnati to meet with the leader of the Knights, a man named George W. Bickley, and he would give him the money they had raised.

After the growers left, I cleared the platters and washed the cups and dishes in the kitchen. Ada, the cook, packed up the leftover food. Miss Clarissa came in and stood beside me. She asked, "Rebecca, you know I don't like it when my father and brother whip slaves. I don't see any need to be so cruel. But I can't imagine this plantation without slaves to work the fields, can you? Can you imagine being free, Rebecca?"

I didn't know how to answer; I didn't know my own mind then. My pa and my ma were slaves, I was born into slavery and I thought my children would be slaves, too. I believed it was the way it had to be. But then I thought about Grower Brown's cruelty. He whipped slaves and worked them so hard that they fell to the ground. I wanted to believe there was a place where that would not happen. I kept drying the dishes and putting them away, but my mind was busy thinking about a world without slavery.

That night I told my ma and pa what I had heard at the meeting. I asked them, "Why aren't runaways free, even in the North?"

My pa looked sad. He said, "In the northern states, a white man cannot buy, sell or own slaves, but runaways can be captured and sent back to their owners. It's only if runaways get as far as Canada that they can't be returned to their owners. But Canada is a long way north."

"Master Jeff said white people in the North help runaways," I said. "He said abolitionists hide runaways, feed them and smuggle them into Canada."

My pa shook his head. "Rebecca, I have never met a white man I could trust. It's hard for me to believe white people will help runaways if it might bring trouble to them. I've heard they can be fined or put in jail if they help runaway slaves."

That night as I went to bed, my pa said, "We're lucky to be together as a family. For some slaves, freedom is something they hunger for, but not me. I never want to be a runaway. Running is too dangerous."

My ma agreed. "Yes, we're lucky to be together. Your father and I get to watch you grow up, Rebecca, and I hope someday you'll help Miss Clarissa raise her children." My pa wrapped his arms around her.

As I fell asleep, I thought about Moses, a black woman who led runaways to freedom in Canada. People called her Moses because in the book of Exodus in the Bible, it was Moses who led his people out of Egypt to the Promised Land. Moses came to Grower Brown's plantation from time to time. If she came again, would any slaves follow her?

A few days later, I was stirring a pot of corn mush on the stove when Miss Clarissa came into the kitchen. Her eyes were red from crying, but when I asked her what was wrong, she said she couldn't tell me. I asked, "Why not?" She shook her head and I knew then that something bad was going to happen, and I figured it was going to happen to me or my family.

I begged her to tell me what was wrong and finally she broke down. "My pa is going to sell your father Obadiah down the river. A grower in the Mississippi Delta needs slaves to work on his rice plantation and he's offering a good price."

Miss Clarissa started to cry and soon I was crying, too. I wanted to run into the fields right away to tell my pa and ma what my friend had told me, but I had to stay in the kitchen and keep working. I had to wait for them to come in from the fields.

That night I told my parents what Miss Clarissa had said. My pa and ma were quiet, as if they didn't have the breath to speak. My pa sat on a stool, his back bent, his head in his hands. My ma stood by him and there was a long silence.

"Obadiah," my ma said, "what do you think we should do? Do you think we should run away?"

He shook his head. "No, I remember Old Foss. He ran away but Grower Brown found him and brought him back. Foss had been whipped so hard, he might as well have been dead. In the end, Grower Brown sold him down the river but I doubt Old Foss lived to see the plantation he was headed for."

My ma asked, "But what else can we do? If we don't run away, Rebecca and I will never see you again. Maybe we'll have to go with Moses, all of us. Maybe there's no other way."

My pa sat in silence for a long time. My ma put a hand on his shoulder and waited for him to speak. Finally he said, "No, it's too dangerous to run away. Master Jeff said there are people in the North who will help runaways, but in the South, we know that runaways are caught and whipped. You can't reach the North without passing through the South. I will go to the Mississippi Delta while you two stay here. Maybe someday I can make my way back." My pa lowered his head and covered his face with his hands. Tears flowed through his calloused fingers.

Never before had I seen my pa so troubled. Something in the way he looked made me speak and I heard a voice that was not my own. "Pa, if you let Grower Brown sell you down the river, you will be dead to me. I will run away from here, even if you won't."

My pa looked startled. "What are you saying, child?"

"If you let yourself be sold down the river, I will go with Moses. I will not stay here. There will be no life for me on this plantation." I was surprised by the sound of my own voice. Where did those harsh words come from?

My ma looked at me with worried eyes. I waited for her to speak but she just stared at me for a long time. Then, shaking her head, she smiled. She knew my pa well. He often said he would walk on burning coals for me. Would he become a runaway?

My pa stood up and hugged me. "Rebecca, when you came out of your mother's womb, I never knew what a force of nature had been born. Maybe the Lord is speaking through the mouth of a child, an innocent child, and telling me what I need to do."

He walked to the window and looked out. "You know

I won't let you go north alone, Rebecca. No, I won't do that. My pa and his pa before him were slaves, but maybe we're finished being slaves. Maybe we can make it to Canada; maybe we can make it to freedom."

My ma said, "So it's decided. We'll go with Moses."

CHAPTER TWO

Stepping into
the River

⧗

NOW WE HAD TO WAIT until Moses made her way to Grower Brown's. There was no telling when she would come but we knew what would happen when she did. One night there would be a knock on the door and there Moses would be. She would go from shack to shack, telling the slaves that they could follow her to freedom. She was a small woman, not much taller than me, but she was fearless, and there were always slaves who believed in her and followed her.

Moses would say, "Who's coming on the train to freedom? Who's riding the Underground Railroad?"

This time, when Moses asked, my pa, my ma and I would answer, "We are. We want to ride the train from slavery to freedom, from midnight to dawn."

Night after night, we waited for the knock on the door. We put out the word among other slaves that our family wanted to ride the Underground Railroad. There was a grapevine where word was passed from slave to slave, from plantation to plantation. We knew we could trust the grapevine; slaves would never tell growers who was planning to run away. We prayed. We prayed day and night that Moses would come before my pa was sent down the river. We waited and waited yet Moses did not come.

Even so, our prayers must have reached heaven because the agent who was going to ship my pa to Mississippi got sick. He sent word to Grower Brown that he couldn't travel for some weeks.

We kept praying. Then one night, there was a knock on our door. It was Moses! She said, "I heard you're ready to ride the Underground Railroad. It's best for me to keep moving so we'll leave tonight." Moses was a tiny woman but she stood as though she were ten feet tall, strong and proud, with a revolver tucked in her belt.

Moses told us to pack cornbread in a calico bag and to wrap blankets around our shoulders. We left the shack quietly and followed Moses into the darkness. Grower Brown's dogs were barking in the pen. The dogs were mean and the barking sent shivers down my spine. When we looked back at the big house, we could see by the light on the table that Grower Brown was sitting on the veranda drinking whiskey. We hoped that it would be morning before he learned that we had run away. We crawled through the grass until the ground became soft and muddy, and we knew we'd reached the swamp. Then we followed Moses into the murky water and walked through the swamp to reach the river.

There were snakes in the swamp and I was scared. Part of me wanted to run out of there, back to our shack, but a bigger part of me never wanted to go back. My pa reached out and took my hand. We were on the Underground Railroad, we had put our faith in Moses, and we had no choice but to follow her.

Soon I heard the gentle current of the river, the water gurgling over the rocks. Moses stepped into the river and reached back to help me. We stepped deeper and deeper into the water.

Moses whispered, "We've got to wade in the water or the dogs will get our scent." It was hard going. Although the current was weak, the rocks under our feet were slippery. Sometimes I fell but my pa lifted me up.

After we'd walked in the river for some time, I leaned into my ma and said, "I can't keep going. I need to rest." I had been a house slave and my legs weren't strong.

Ma said, "Moses and I worked in the fields, so we're almost as strong as a man. You were a house slave—why, I thought that was a good thing, but tonight I wish you had worked in the fields. You have to keep walking, Rebecca."

I knew my ma was right. We walked and walked until the sun came up. Moses stopped and pointed to the north. "There's an island there where we can hide and the dogs can't follow us. We can rest in a big hollowed-out tree, but before we sleep, we have to build a raft." We looked at her, puzzled. She said, "The water runs deep on the other side of the island. If Grower Brown follows us there, we'll need a raft to get away."

Moses smiled. "I don't leave anything to chance. What if we woke up and the growers and their dogs were on the riverbank? We'd be trapped out there. That's why we're going to build a raft out of deadfall trees and leave it on the other side of the island, out of sight. Then we can climb onto that raft and get away if need be."

When we reached the island, we grabbed onto branches and pulled ourselves out of the river. We wrung the water out of our clothes and picked leeches off our legs. Then we looked for logs, logs that weren't too rotten to float. While my pa carried the logs to the far side of the island, Moses and my ma tore strips from the bottom of their skirts. Pa lashed four big logs across two shorter logs with those strips of cloth. The raft was small but it would carry us downriver if Grower Brown and his men came to search the island.

We huddled together in the hollow tree where Moses led us. It was damp and musty but I was so tired that I quickly fell asleep. I slept all through the rest of the day and would have kept sleeping all through the night but my ma woke me up. "Rebecca, it's time to get moving. It's dark." We were about to start walking in the river, when Moses raised her finger to her lips and motioned for us to hide again.

We stopped and listened. Men were shouting and dogs were barking on the riverbank. We heard Grower Brown shout, "Men, we've got to cross to that island. Those slaves could be hiding there."

Master Jeff answered, "Let's go back and get some horses so we can ride across the river. I'm not partial to walking in water that's full of snakes—and gators, too."

"Let's hurry and get those horses then," Grower Brown said. "I'm betting that those slaves didn't run away on their own. This may be our chance to catch Moses!"

I was shaking with fear. My ma took my hand; she was trembling, too. We looked at Moses, waiting for her to show us what to do. As soon as the men left the river-bank, Moses quietly crawled out of the hollow tree and started running to the raft. My pa crawled out of our hiding spot and followed her. Ma and I, we followed, too.

CHAPTER THREE

The Bayou of Death

⚜

WHEN WE REACHED the raft, Moses whispered, "We're going to take that raft and drift downstream to the Bayou of Death. We'll hide for a piece in the bayou and let the gators and water moccasins guard us. Grower Brown and his men can ride their horses in the river but not in the bayou; with all the bushes and tree roots, the horses would be likely to break their legs. And we know Master Jeff is scared to walk in the water. He'll be in no rush to search for us in the bayou, not any time soon."

My pa frowned. "Isn't the bayou to the south?"

"Yes," Moses said. "Sometimes on the Railroad you have to go south to get north."

Pa climbed onto the raft. The logs sank in the water but they held his weight. Then my ma climbed on, then me and last Moses. The raft barely held us afloat and my pa shifted his weight to keep us balanced. My pa whispered, "I know the Bayou of Death. When I was a boy, I played there on Sundays."

Moses used a pole to steer us into the current. We all crouched down, with our faces just above the water. Moses told us to keep looking for a small creek that ran between the river and the bayou. Moonlight fell on the water and we hoped there was enough light to find that creek. The raft followed the river, twisting and turning. We sat up now but held each other tight so we wouldn't fall into the water.

Like my pa, I knew about the Bayou of Death. On Sundays, field workers from the plantation would throw logs across one creek, then another. The boys would dare each other to wade into the water of the bayou alone, but no one would because they were all afraid. So in the end, all of them would go in together. Sometimes they brought back snakes to scare us girls. My ma said I should never go near that bayou, not because of the snakes, but because, from time to time, runaway slaves hid there. She didn't want me near trouble.

One summer day Miss Clarissa had asked me to come and play in an old log cabin across the river from the bayou. Her granddaddy had built the cabin when he started clearing land to plant cotton. She carried some china dishes and a blanket and I carried a basket of food. Now I remembered that, as we ate our picnic, I told Miss Clarissa that runaway slaves hid in the bayou.

Had Miss Clarissa told her father or her brother that runaways hid there? She couldn't have known that there would be any harm in that. How could she have known that one day I would be a runaway hiding in the bayou? I didn't know whether I should tell Moses what I had told Miss Clarissa, but Moses was busy guiding the raft downstream, and I decided not to tell her, at least, not for now.

Pointing to a narrow opening along the riverbank, Moses said softly, "There. We go in there." My pa knelt, took the pole from Moses and pushed the raft into the creek. Moses said, "Push deeper until we find a patch of dry ground. Then we can get some sleep."

Overhead, moss hung on the cypress trees and made the dark night darker. It was quiet except for the sound of frogs croaking. As the raft struggled through the weeds and tangled roots, I knew that I had to tell Moses what I had told Miss Clarissa. I said that Miss Clarissa and I used play in a log cabin across the river from the bayou. It was a secret place where we could play without her father knowing. From there, we could see the field hands crossing the creek into the bayou. One day I had told Miss Clarissa that runaway slaves hid in the bayou.

My ma said, "Oh, no, Rebecca, you should never have told her that. Now they'll be looking for us here." My face burned with the shame I felt.

Moses said, "Take this pole, child, and push us deeper into the bayou. There is no going back now, whatever Miss Clarissa did or did not choose to tell her brother and her pa. Put your back into it. We've got to get to the heart of the bayou."

I knew Moses was right; there was no going back. Moses was not only strong but wise, and I knew I would learn much from her as we made our way to freedom.

We found a dry spot in the middle of the bayou. In the darkness, it was hard to get off the raft and I slipped on the muddy shore. My pa pulled me up and carried me to dry land where we sat and ate the cornbread that my ma had carried in the calico bag. It was soggy but we ate every last bit of it. Moses told us to try to sleep. I rested but could not sleep. The croaking of the frogs was loud and I thought I heard snakes and gators sliding in and out of the water.

My pa hugged me. "I'd rather be on the run—even with the gators—than a broken man under the whip of Grower Brown. Try to sleep, Rebecca."

My ma put her head on one of my pa's shoulders and I put my head on the other. Moses broke the silence, "There's nothing to do but wait. We may have to wait two, three days until Grower Brown and his men give up and start looking farther north. He's probably hired patrollers to look for us and those patrollers will want the money he's offered them for our capture. I just hope that Miss Clarissa didn't tell her pa about the bayou."

Soon after, and out of the quiet of the night, we heard singing. Moses held her finger to her lips and we all listened. I recognized the voice and the song. "Moses, it's my friend Miss Clarissa. She's come to help us." I was about to call out to my friend when Moses put her hand over my mouth.

Moses looked at me and shook her head. "Rebecca, runaways don't have any white friends who live on plantations. Hush, child."

The sound of Miss Clarissa's voice got stronger as she walked along the creek. Moses said, "Her father and brother may be using the girl to trick us. We can't take any chances."

Miss Clarissa stopped singing and started talking. "I don't know if you are in the bayou, Rebecca, but I'm leaving two bags of food for you. If you are in there, you must be hungry. I had to come. I had to come even though I was afraid because I need to warn you. Rebecca, you and your pa and your ma—you're all in great danger. If you are in there, you must leave the bayou right away."

I started to move toward Miss Clarissa, but Moses grabbed my arm and whispered, "Wait."

Miss Clarissa went on, "I want to tell you what happened. If my father and brother find you here, you need to know that I didn't betray you."

She paused to catch her breath. "Patrollers searched the island with dogs today. The dogs picked up your scent in a hollow tree but the trail went cold on the far shore. My father said you couldn't swim because he thinks slaves sink like stones in the water. My brother said the only way to escape from the island was on a raft and that raft would carry you downstream to the Bayou of Death."

As we listened to what Miss Clarissa was saying, Moses relaxed her grip on my arm. "My father said he and his men will search the bayou tonight and, if they don't find you, they'll ride upriver in the morning. I had to warn you, even though my father will be very angry if he finds out. Before I came, I went into the kitchen and asked Ada to fill some sacks with food. At first Ada looked puzzled, then she smiled and realized that it was food for you. Then, out of the corner of my eye, I saw Tom, the son of Grower Timothy. I hid in the pantry and waited for him to leave before I slipped out the back door. When I got to the log cabin, I started singing the song we used to sing together, Rebecca, so you would know it was me coming to warn you."

She paused, out of breath. "You must flee tonight, Rebecca. When you reach freedom, ask someone to write a letter to me so I will know that you are safe. I'm your friend. I will always be your friend." As she walked back to the big house, I heard her crying.

Moses said, "Well, child, I reckon I was wrong about your friend Miss Clarissa. Thank the Lord I was wrong. Obadiah, will you cross the creek and get the food?" My pa disappeared into the darkness and was back soon. We tore off chunks of bread and ate them hungrily.

"Now, let's get these tired bodies back on the raft,"

Moses said. "Deborah, hold the food as high as you can so it doesn't get wet. We have to move, and we have to move fast, but before we go, I'll cover our tracks."

Moses reached into a sack of food, took out a ham, and cut off a large slice. She stamped her feet on the marshy ground and pulled her kerchief off her head. She wrapped the ham in the kerchief and left it in the mud. Then we all climbed onto the raft.

She chuckled. "When Grower Brown sees those scraps of cloth, he'll think the gators got us." She shoved her pole into the mud and pushed the raft off the bank. As we left, we saw a gator swimming toward the ham. In a moment, all that was left were scraps of cloth from the kerchief and the slithering marks of the gator's claws.

We passed from the creek into the river. Through the night, we moved north, upstream. It was hard, hard work, even for a strong man like my pa. I thought to myself, "We'll never get upstream by morning." I looked at my pa and saw that his face was glistening with sweat. But, as he looked back at me, his lips curled into a smile.

He spoke softly, "Rebecca, you were right when you said we had to run away. I've been waiting for freedom all my life without knowing it."

Just before the sun came up, we stopped and went

ashore. The raft slipped back downstream, twisting and turning in the gentle current. Moses told us to hide in a thick clump of bushes in the cool shade. We ate some of the food Miss Clarissa had brought us, and my ma and I tried to sleep while Moses and my pa sat up and watched over us.

After Grower Brown and the patrollers searched the bayou, they would search for us along this stretch of the river. I hoped we were safe, hidden in the bushes.

When my ma and I woke up, the sun was going down. My ma asked Moses, "What do we do next? When do we get on the Railroad?"

Moses laughed. "Deborah, honey, we *are* on the Railroad. The next station is the Pickerings' farm. But before we get there, we've got to stop and pick up one more passenger for this train. Tonight we're going to Grower Timothy's plantation. Right now we've got to start walking, fast but quiet. The last place a grower thinks to look for runaways is another man's plantation."

CHAPTER FOUR

My Uncle Josiah

⤟⤞

WE REACHED GROWER TIMOTHY's plantation just as the sun was beginning to rise. We were more frightened than tired because we knew Grower Timothy was as mean as Grower Brown.

Moses knocked on the door of a slave shack. When the door opened, we were surprised to see my uncle Josiah, my pa's brother. Moses clapped her hands. "Obadiah, I wanted to surprise you. Josiah is going to ride the Underground Railroad with you."

We hugged one another and talked until we heard a

loud bell, a bell that called the slaves to work every morning. Uncle Josiah hurried to the fields while we hid out of sight of the window in a corner of the shack. We did not dare to look but we pictured what was happening outside—the slaves coming and going, the overseers shouting at them to hurry, the chickens clucking and the dogs barking.

The grapevine was busy that day, carrying news from slave to slave. The house slaves listened to Grower Timothy and his son as they talked about us runaways and they carried news to the fields, along with food and water. They told Uncle Josiah what Grower Timothy had said, and that night Uncle Josiah carried that news back to us.

"Last night Grower Brown sent his patrollers into the Bayou of Death," Uncle Josiah said. "But, of course, they didn't find you runaways. He thinks the gators got you. But Grower Timothy's son, Tom, has a different opinion. He was staying at Grower Brown's last night and he saw Miss Clarissa heading to the bayou. He thinks she warned you that the patrollers were headed that way. Grower Timothy knows I'm your brother, Obadiah, and he knows I'm not afraid to run away. After my wife and little son died of the fever last spring, I have nothing to lose. I'm ready to ride the Underground Railroad and he knows it. He'll be watching me."

Moses said, "That's exactly what I want Grower Timothy to do, to watch this shack. Under the bed, there is an empty well. A long time ago slaves dug a tunnel there that leads to the woods. Now that it's dark, we can make our way down the well and through the tunnel. A driver will be waiting for us in the woods."

Then Moses and Uncle Josiah lifted the bed out of the way and began scraping away the dirt. When Moses lifted up two old boards, we smelled the mustiness of the old well. We heard footsteps and Uncle Josiah whispered, "Grower Timothy and his men are starting to surround my shack."

Moses said, "It's time to go." She hurried down a wooden ladder that was set in the old well and motioned for me to follow her, then my ma, my pa and Uncle Josiah. When we reached the bottom of the well, Moses lit a candle, and in the flickering light I could see a tunnel, a tunnel just big enough for us to crawl through.

"Wait here," Moses said. "I've got some business to do in the shack." She climbed back up the ladder, carrying the candle in one hand. At the top of the ladder, she held the candle to some kindling. We saw the fire and smelled smoke. Moses left the kindling burning on the floor of the shack and pulled the boards back over the hole.

The tunnel was narrow and low so I had to crawl on my hands and knees. Moses said, "Now, child, just pretend you are a little mouse crawling through the earth. Go as fast as you can!" I put one hand down, then the other, and kept crawling. I kept crawling until I saw moonlight and knew I had come to the end of the tunnel. I climbed up a log ladder into a small clearing.

I thought we had gone a long way from Uncle Josiah's shack, but when I looked through the trees, the burning shack was a stone's throw away. Sparks jumped from shack to shack, and Grower Timothy shouted for his slaves to pour water on the flames. I turned away; I never wanted to see Grower Timothy again.

Uncle Josiah stood silent, watching the fire destroy the shack where he had lived with his wife and son. He spoke in a low, soft voice, "Goodbye, my dear wife. I must leave you and our son here, but we'll meet in the next world." He wiped tears from his eyes and my pa put a hand on his shoulder. "Amen," he said.

We bent low and ran into the woods. In a small clearing, we saw a man standing beside a wagon. Moses said, "This is Ezekiel and he's been waiting for us. Josiah, you

know Ezekiel. He's a slave on Grower Timothy's plantation and I'm hoping he won't be missed in the confusion
of the fire."

Ezekiel laughed, "I hope I won't be missed, too, Moses.
But I'll drive you and these good people in any case."

"Where are we going?" my ma asked.

Moses said, "To North Carolina."

"I like the sound of that word 'north,'" my pa said.

After we climbed into the wagon, Ezekiel put bags of
feed around us and covered us with planks. Then he
loaded more feed on top of the boards. The bags were so
dusty I started to choke, and Moses whispered for me to
hold my breath. We had to stay quiet as we crossed a
wide lane on Grower Timothy's plantation, a lane that
led to the main road.

We moved slowly and quietly until we reached the
road. Grower Timothy and his men were so busy with
the fire that they didn't notice Ezekiel driving the wagon.
We stopped by a creek and washed the dust out of our
mouths. After Ezekiel told us to get back in the wagon,
he again packed the bags of feed tight around us, then
covered us with the planks of wood and more feed. Now
we moved along at a fast pace, bouncing as the wagon
jolted along the rough road. My pa tried to hold tight to

me so I wouldn't be thrown against the hard wooden boards above and below us. Even so, I felt bruises rising on my arms, knees and forehead.

We heard Ezekiel talking to the two horses pulling the wagon, talking to them as though they were people. "You've got to get these runaways up the Railroad fast. Far from Grower Timothy's. Then you and I will hurry back to the plantation before that man even knows we were gone. Giddy-up!"

When Ezekiel fell silent, Moses sang softly. "Ezekiel saw the wheel, way up in the middle of the sky. The big wheel turned by faith, the little wheel turned by the grace of God. A wheel in a wheel, way up in the middle of the sky." The words were familiar because field hands sang this song when they picked cotton.

I closed my eyes. My body ached but the rumble of the wheels was a comfort to me. Every turn of the wheels brought us closer to Canada.

Without warning, the wagon lurched to a stop. I held my breath and my pa hugged me tight. I heard a man's voice, a voice I did not know. "You there, boy, what are you doing out at this time of night? You know, south of here, two growers lost some slaves."

"Oh, I didn't hear anything about that," Ezekiel

replied. "Me, I'm just taking this wagon to my master's son, up near the border. Master, he told me to drive this feed up there tonight. I begged him, I said, 'Master, I'll do it first thing in the morning' but he said, 'No, you'll do it now.' I don't like driving at night because there are ghosts and spirits out here in the woods. Master doesn't care if they get me or not."

The man scoffed. "We're looking for runaways, not ghosts. Some say those runaways were eaten by gators; others say they all burned in a fire on Grower Timothy's plantation. But some say they're alive and on the run. There's a reward for those runaways—big money for a man they call Moses." Frightened though I was, I wanted to laugh when I heard him call Moses a man.

Another man said gruffly, "I need to see what you've got in that wagon."

Ezekiel said, "Go ahead. You can look for runaways but you won't find any in this wagon. I don't much care for runaways, I don't. They make trouble for all us slaves."

The men climbed onto the wagon and poked pitchforks into the feed bags that lay on top of the planks. I prayed that the wood would hold. A splinter cut my leg and I bit my lip so I wouldn't cry out. I squirmed closer to the side of the wagon.

The men jumped down and one of them said, "Okay, no runaways here. Get on your way."

Ezekiel said, "If you fellows are travelling north, I'd be grateful for your company on this dark, lonely road."

"We're not out here to keep you company, boy. We've got to catch those runaways."

Ezekiel said, "I best be going then. Master will be some upset if I don't get that feed delivered by the time the sun rises."

"Giddy-up," he said, and the horses started trotting down the road. We were travelling again and we travelled all night long, hour after hour, until we reached North Carolina.

CHAPTER FIVE

The Zigzag Route

I AWOKE IN BRIGHT daylight and all was quiet. I didn't see Ezekiel or the wagon. Had he abandoned us? I looked at Moses and whispered, "Where is Ezekiel? Why did he leave us here?"

Moses said, "He went back to the plantation. He had to be back before morning so Grower Timothy wouldn't know he'd been gone."

Moses pointed to a farmhouse across the road from us. Through the thick trees that lined the road, I saw a white woman hanging laundry on a clothesline. She wore a plain black bonnet and a long black dress. She un-pegged a quilt, a blue quilt with bright yellow stars in the pattern of the Big Dipper. She shook the quilt, folded it and put it in her laundry basket. Then she hung up a quilt with blocks of bright colour in a zigzag pattern. After she looked up and down the road, she went about her chores, feeding the chickens and sweeping the wide porch that lined the front of her house.

Moses pointed to the clothesline. "Did you see that blue quilt, child, the one with the Big Dipper? That quilt says it's safe to go to the house. But the one Missus Pickering just hung up, the one on the line now, it's called the Drunkard's Path and it means danger. We need to wait and watch what happens next. The patrollers are likely to come this way."

Moses looked at me. "Missus Pickering is a Quaker. You know who Quakers are, child?"

I remembered something Miss Clarissa told me last year. She had met a woman in Henderson's Dry Goods Store, a woman dressed all in black just like Missus Pickering. When the woman spoke to the clerk, she talked as though she were reading words in the Bible. Miss Clarissa's father started scolding the cook Ada, and the woman told him to stop. "One day," she said, "all slaves will be free." Grower Brown told his daughter that the Quaker woman didn't belong in the South.

I answered Moses, "I know that Quakers think slaves should be free."

Moses smiled. "That's right. Another name for Quakers is Friends and, for sure, they're friends to runaways. Without freed blacks, Friends, Unitarians and the abolitionists of other faiths, there would be no Underground Railroad. And without the Railroad, we could not find our way to freedom. It's as plain and simple as that."

My ma said, "Moses, that woman is white. How can we trust her?"

Moses looked her straight in the eye. "Yes, Deborah, she's as white as that bleached sheet hanging on the clothesline. But we can trust her; we have to trust her."

My ma looked down. "I've never trusted a white woman in my life. Miss Clarissa is a friend to Rebecca but she is a child. I've never had reason to trust any grown-up white person and I'm not sure I can."

There was a hush. Moses reached out and took my ma's hand in her own sinewy one. "Deborah, I understand. I certainly do understand, because there was a time when I felt that way, too. But you have to have faith in the Underground Railroad."

In the heat of the day, flies swarmed around us, annoying us with their buzzing and their biting. Suddenly, Moses raised her finger to her lips and pushed us down, deep into the underbrush. Two patrollers on horseback rode up to Missus Pickering.

"Ma'am, have you seen any runaways?" one of the men asked. "They're armed and dangerous."

Missus Pickering looked at the man and said in a kindly voice, "Can I offer thee a drink of lemonade? Thee must be thirsty."

Just like the woman Miss Clarissa had met, she sounded like she was reading from the Holy Book, the Bible. I wondered if all Quakers talked that way.

The men took off their hats and said they would be grateful for a drink, so Missus Pickering went into the house. When she returned, and handed the men their lemonade, the taller one said, "Ma'am, we thank you for the drink but we are going to search your house, your cellar and your barn." The men searched the yard, too, but did not come near the thicket where we were hidden.

The men shook their heads. "We didn't find any runaways this time, but we're going to keep an eye on you and all the other Quakers between here and the Mason–Dixon Line. We know you Friends like to help runaways, but helping them is against the law. You remember that."

Then he sternly warned her. "If we find you or your husband harbouring runaways, there'll be trouble. We'll burn down your barns."

Missus Pickering smiled and said calmly, "Would thee like more lemonade?"

The men shook their heads no, and turned their horses toward the road. As they rode away, we heard the woman say, "May the Lord bless thee and keep thee. And may He forgive thee for thy sins."

A few minutes later a man drove a horse and wagon into the yard. He was dressed in a plain, dusty black suit. He came straight toward the thicket where we were hiding, and said, "My brethren and sisters, please come into my home." He bowed his head and said, "As it says in the Gospel of Matthew, 'For I was hungry and you gave me food, I was thirsty and you gave me drink, I was a stranger and you welcomed me.' You are most welcome here."

His wife smiled at us. "As my husband said, thee are most welcome in our home. My name is Mary and my husband's name is Samuel, Samuel Pickering."

Mister Pickering said, "There is a hidden room at the top of the stairs. You will be safe there."

He led us inside and up steep stairs to a landing with a large pine wardrobe. Missus Pickering pushed the clothes aside and opened a small door in the back of the wardrobe. She said, "Thee must stay in the hidden room, for the patrollers may be back at any time."

Mister Pickering said, "Yes, please wait here. I will be off now to the next house on the Underground Railroad. We will plan a way to carry you towards freedom. The patrollers are the biggest danger you face but we must also be mindful of the coming winter."

Uncle Josiah waited for Mister Pickering to leave before shaking his head. "I never thought I'd see a day where white folks would invite us into their home to protect us from patrollers."

My pa nodded. "And I never thought I'd see a day where I'd be running away from slavery. I am thankful, Rebecca, that you set us on the road to freedom."

The hidden room was dark and narrow, the air was hot and still, but we were grateful to be safe. Missus Pickering went downstairs to fetch food and water for us. I sank to the floor, too weary to stand.

Moses said, "Mister Pickering will find a safe way to move us to the next stop. The Underground Railroad can have a lot of twists and turns, but trusted conductors like Mister Pickering will help us find our way north."

My ma asked, "Where will we go from here? What's north of here?"

Uncle Josiah sighed. "Seems like we can't go north, because that's where the patrollers are looking for us."

Moses grunted. "Yes, we may have to go east, west or even south just now. But at the end of the day, we will go north. Usually I go straight north and cross the Mason–Dixon Line at the border of Delaware. Then I go through Philadelphia and New York City—but not this time. Too many patrollers will be watching that route."

I asked, "What is the Mason–Dixon Line?"

Moses said, "North of that line, white folks cannot own, buy or sell slaves, but south of that line they can. The line is part of the Compromise of 1850 when the federal government tried to make peace between those in the South who wanted slavery and those in the North who didn't."

Missus Pickering brought us more water. The heat in the hidden room was rising.

Moses said, "Soon we'll be wishing we had some of this heat to keep us warm. Rebecca, do you know what winter's like in the North?"

I shook my head.

"Well," said Moses, "let me tell you about winter. The

cold is so cold it will make your teeth chatter. There's snow that comes down like cotton falling out of the sky and covers everything—the houses and the roads, the trees and the fields. The streams and rivers, they turn to ice. The ice is as hard as rock and you can walk straight across a river. Can you imagine that?"

Moses continued, "Yes, winter in the North is some cold, but North is where freedom lies. There are lots of ways to go north but all of them are cold at this time of year."

Moses knew we were all worried that the patrollers might come back so she kept talking. "Oh, yes, there are as many ways to go north as there are colours in the rainbow. One slave, he put himself in a box three feet long and two feet wide and mailed himself up North. Now he goes by the name of Henry Box Brown. When they took Henry out of that box, two big men had to pull him straight again."

Moses laughed and we laughed with her. Our fear didn't weigh so heavy on our minds just then.

"Another way to go north is to take a ship out of Charleston, South Carolina, or Norfolk, Virginia. William and Ellen Craft, they escaped from a plantation in Georgia and got on a ship."

On the plantation I had heard many people's stories

about crossing the sea from Africa. Slaves were forced onto ships and chained together, the chains wrapped around posts in the holds, deep down in the ships. "How did William and Ellen travel to freedom on a ship?" I wanted to know.

Moses chuckled, "Ellen, her people were from Africa but she was as white as Grower Brown himself."

I had seen slaves who were white, brown, black and every colour in between. I knew that the growers fancied the fair-skinned women and had children with them, but the children of those women, they were slaves just like the rest of us. It didn't matter what the colour of their skin was, and it didn't matter who fathered them. "I know about slaves with white skin," I said. "But how did Ellen and William stay out of chains on that ship?"

Moses said, "Oh, those slaves, they outwitted their masters. For a long time, they thought and thought about how to escape. Then one night the Lord spoke to Ellen and told her to dress up like a white grower. She did just that and William pretended to be her slave. Ellen, she stayed in a stateroom while William, he stayed with the slaves in the hold."

I asked Moses, "What's a stateroom?"

"Child, it's a fancy room on a ship, with a soft bed to

sleep on and warm blankets and a pretty little round window that looks out on the water."

I tried to picture it—a slave in a stateroom. Moses said, "Ellen and William nearly got caught because Ellen had to sign papers when she boarded the ship, and she didn't know how to read or write. A white man took pity on her and did the writing for Ellen, never imagining he was helping a runaway. Eight days later, they landed in Boston. Unfortunately, the federal marshals were there looking for them, so Ellen and William went on across the ocean to England. England is a place like Canada where slavery is forbidden by law."

Moses suddenly went quiet and rolled onto the floor where she lay still, as if dead. My ma called her name but Moses didn't wake up. My ma knelt over her and felt for her breath. "She's breathing but she's breathing rough."

Moses slept for such a long time that we were scared. We didn't know whether we should call Missus Pickering or not. We prayed that Moses would wake up. Then, as quickly as she had fallen asleep, she awoke, blinking her eyes. It seemed she had no idea where she was or how long she had slept.

I felt bad because I'd been worried about Moses but, even more, I'd been worried about my family and myself.

Without Moses, how could we follow the Underground Railroad? Only Moses knew the conductors; only Moses knew the routes and how to escape the dangers along the way.

Moses sat up. "I'm sorry I scared all of you. Sometimes I have these sleeping spells. When I was a young girl on a plantation in Maryland, people called me by a different name—Minty. I was a field slave and, one day when I was husking corn, an overseer thought the slave working beside me was too slow and he started whipping him. The slave made a run for it, but the overseer ran after him and cornered him in a shed. Without even thinking, I followed them.

"The overseer, he shouted, 'Minty, help me catch that slave!' But there was no way I was going to help him. Instead, when the slave ran out of the shed, I blocked the doorway. That white overseer, he was so mad, he picked up a brick and threw it at the man, but it hit me instead —right on the head. I didn't wake up for days. Ever since then, from time to time, I have these sleeping spells. But don't you worry, I always wake up."

We heard the back of the wardrobe open, and Missus Pickering bent low and brought us porridge and fresh water. She looked at us with worry in her eyes. "When

Samuel returns, I pray thee will be able to move to the next station. My husband should be back soon."

We stayed in the dark, crowded room and waited. Not long after Missus Pickering went back downstairs, we heard men's voices. The patrollers were back. Missus Pickering welcomed them into her home but said, "Thee are looking in the wrong place, for thee will not find slaves here."

"Ma'am, I hope you're telling the truth. Those runaways are dangerous."

"Thee will never find slaves in a house blessed by God," Missus Pickering answered.

The man asked abruptly, "Where is your husband?"

Missus Pickering said that Mister Pickering had gone to town to find a buyer for their corn.

The patrollers rode off, leaving us feeling even more worried than before. What had happened to Mister Pickering? We needed to keep moving north. Missus Pickering waited some time before she came up the stairs and sat on the floor beside us. She knew we were very frightened.

Moses said, "Missus Pickering, thank you for lying to the patrollers, even though you are a religious woman."

Missus Pickering smiled. "I did not lie. There are no

slaves in a house blessed by God, because in God's eyes, there are no slaves."

Soon after, Missus Pickering hurried downstairs when we heard a rider approaching the house. We were worried that the patrollers were back. This time, they might find the hidden room behind the wardrobe. We were relieved to hear Mister Pickering greet his wife. "Mary, I have returned. I trust all is well here?"

A few minutes later, both the Pickerings came up the stairs, bringing us bread and a pot of beans. Hungry as we were, we did not eat until Mister Pickering told us his plan for the next step on our journey.

Mister Pickering said, "Brethren and sisters, I am concerned for you. You have enraged the growers. In their minds, you have made trouble, like a stick poked into a beehive. The roads north are not safe to travel."

Moses looked at Mister Pickering. "If we are in the middle of a beehive, we can't stay here much longer. We don't want harm to come to you kind folks. I've seen too many barns burned because growers hate you Quakers. They hate all abolitionists."

Mister Pickering shook his head. "I have talked with other Quakers and we agree that you will be hunted without mercy between here and Delaware. But there will be fewer patrollers if you go west to Memphis, Tennessee. Tennessee is a slave state but Quakers there will help you board a steamboat that will carry you up the Mississippi River to St. Louis, Missouri. We have found a quadroon, a fair-skinned slave, who wishes to join you on the Underground Railroad. Her name is Delilah. She will pretend to be your mistress on the steamboat."

Moses said, "It is a daring plan, but remember the story of Ellen and William Craft? Ellen was able to pass as a white grower, and she and William escaped."

CHAPTER SIX

Travelling as the Dead

❧

A FEW NIGHTS LATER, Mister Pickering came up to the hidden room and said, "Brethren and sisters, now is the time for you to flee. You will travel in a most unusual way."

He led us outside where two black horses were hitched to a big black wagon, a hearse. Last spring, when Grower Brown's father died, a hearse like this one had carried the old man's body to the graveyard. Now, a stranger stood beside the wagon. He was dressed in a black suit, like Mister Pickering, and I thought he must be another Quaker. Mister Pickering said, "This is my friend, Daniel, and he has brought this hearse to carry you to the steamboat. There are five coffins with holes cut in the side to help you to breathe. I will drive you myself, and, with the help of God, we will reach Memphis in a week."

My pa helped me into the back of the hearse, opened one coffin and lifted me gently over the side. With my hand, I traced the circles that were cut in the boards. Sap oozed from the freshly cut, rough wood. Pa motioned for me to lie down, then closed the coffin.

We travelled all night. The road was rough, and my body was soon covered with fresh bruises. The scent of the fresh-cut pine was strong and my throat burned. When Mister Pickering found a quiet place in the woods, he stopped the horses and opened the coffins. Then he rested while the rest of us kept watch for patrollers and bounty hunters. Moses said patrollers would be scared of a hearse, a wagon of death, but we kept watch anyway.

I do not know how long we travelled in the hearse. Day was like night and time passed slowly. At last, we came to a farmhouse and Mister Pickering hitched fresh horses to the wagon. The farmer gave us food to eat and water to drink. While we ate, Moses told us stories about the Moses in the Bible. She told us that Moses had a brother Aaron who stayed beside him as he led the Hebrew people to freedom. I hoped that Mister Pickering was like Aaron; I hoped that he would stay with us until we reached Memphis—and beyond.

That night, I woke up with a start because the hearse had stopped moving. Mister Pickering said softly, "We are just outside the town of Chattanooga so we must remain quiet while Moses goes to meet Delilah at the Davis Plantation. This is a good time for you to climb out of the coffins and stretch your legs." I was so stiff I almost fell over but Mister Pickering took my arm and steadied me. "You will find your strength soon, Rebecca," he said kindly.

Moses said, "When I return with Delilah, we'll move on. Be ready."

I wondered whether Moses would bring another coffin for Delilah, but then I remembered that Delilah would be travelling as a white grower. Mister Pickering spread blankets on the ground and we all lay down to sleep. I was happy because I was not sleeping in a pine coffin or in the back of a wagon; I was sleeping under the stars.

When I awoke in the morning, Mister Pickering was pacing up and down in front of the hearse. My pa, my ma and Uncle Josiah stood near him, and everyone looked worried. Moses was missing. She had not returned with Delilah.

Mister Pickering tried to comfort us as he said, "Moses was supposed to return with Delilah last night but, as you can see, they did not come. I am sure that they will join us soon but we must have a plan in case something unexpected has happened. I cannot go to Grower Davis's plantation to inquire about Delilah. Growers don't trust Friends, knowing that we believe slavery to be wrong. We must wait and pray while I think what to do next."

We waited and waited all day and into the night. I feared that Moses had been caught or that she had suffered another sleeping spell. We rested but could not sleep.

In the middle of the night, we heard a noise in the woods, the noise of someone walking through the brush. An owl hooted. Mister Pickering quickly helped us into the coffins. Then he untethered the horses and harnessed them to the hearse so we were ready to flee if need be. I kept my breathing quiet and shallow so I could hear every sound. The noise got louder and we soon heard a man singing as he crashed through the woods. Surely it was not Moses.

Then I heard an owl hooting again. At least I thought

it was an owl. The stranger called out, "Good evening."

Mister Pickering replied, "Good evening, brother."

The man said, "I see that you are on a sad journey."

"Yes," Mister Pickering replied. "I am taking an unfortunate family to Memphis for burial. They were killed in a house fire as the family slept. I seem to have lost my way. Perhaps you can point out the way to Memphis?"

There was silence again and I strained to hear more. Who was this man? He sounded friendly, but why was he out in the woods at this time of night? Was he a patroller?

The man said, "I would be happy to draw you a map. I am familiar with this country although I am from Belleville, a town in Upper Canada. My apologies, I should have introduced myself. My name is Alexander—Alexander Milton Ross. I'm a doctor but I'm also an ornithologist, a scientist who studies birds. I am looking for a rare species of owl that can be found only in this part of Tennessee. Perhaps you heard an owl tonight?"

I heard Mister Pickering laugh. "Brother, I have heard an owl but I think it was you who was hooting. Tell me, are you staying at the Davis Plantation? Has there been any trouble there?"

Doctor Ross answered, "Yes, I'm staying with Grower Davis. I arranged to spend three months in the South, visiting many plantations in my search for the owl. My research will be part of a book. I have published one work, *Ferns and Wildflowers of Canada*, and I am anxious to publish another book about owls."

Mister Pickering again asked, "Was there any trouble on the Davis Plantation? A friend of mine goes there from time to time."

"No, there was no trouble, except for a slave named Delilah. Grower Davis said she stole a chicken although she had stolen nothing. Grower Davis sent her to Ghost Island anyway, saying she had to stay there for five days. The poor soul must be very frightened. I tried to convince Grower Davis that the woman was innocent but he wouldn't listen."

After a long pause, Mister Pickering asked, "Tell me, are there slaves in Canada?"

Doctor Ross said, "Thankfully, there are no slaves because my country is part of the British Empire, and slavery was abolished throughout the Empire in 1834. Before that, I'm sad to say, many people in Canada did have slaves. In 1793, the Lieutenant-Governor of Upper Canada, John Simcoe, passed a law forbidding anyone to bring more slaves into the province, but slaves who were already there remained in bondage."

"And what is your personal opinion about slavery?" Mister Pickering asked.

"I believe slavery is evil," Doctor Ross answered. "I'm sure you have heard of the Underground Railroad, a bridge from slavery to freedom. Canada is the bedrock on which one foot of that bridge rests, so I am proud to say I am a Canadian. Runaway slaves are not always welcomed by white folks in Canada but the law protects their freedom and provides security, to the extent it can."

Doctor Ross continued. "When I was young, I wanted to heal the sick so I became a doctor. Now I want to heal the evil of slavery. Whenever possible, I help slaves who are seeking freedom. They call me the Birdman."

Mister Pickering laughed. "The Birdman? Why do they call you by that name?"

The Birdman replied, "First, I want to ask you whether you are a Friend?"

"Yes," Mister Pickering answered. "I am a Friend, a Quaker."

"Then I have to ask you a question about your religion," Doctor Ross went on. "Do Friends believe in the Christian act of baptism, being dipped in holy water, in order to covenant with God?"

Mister Pickering said, "I can see, Doctor Ross, that

you are a cautious man and you are testing me to make sure that I am indeed a Quaker. Well, let me answer your question. We reject the sacrament of baptism, we pray in silence and we believe that God speaks directly to man."

The Birdman said, "You have convinced me that you are indeed a Quaker. Now I will tell you about my name. Slaves call me the Birdman because I visit many plantations as I search for rare birds. Although I eat and drink with the growers and stay in their large houses, I go to the slave quarters at night. I have good reason to walk out into the darkness in my search for owls. Slaves who seek freedom gather around me and I give them coins, a compass and a map to guide them north. I teach them the call of the owl and other birds so they can signal to one another as they flee. I sincerely wish I could do more."

Mister Pickering said, "Perhaps you can, for I believe that God has sent you to me this night. I am in need of help."

I was frightened. Would Mister Pickering trust this man with our lives? But, if he didn't ask for help, how would we find out what had happened to Moses?

The Birdman said, "If I can be of help, please tell me what I can do."

We lay in our coffins, listening, as Mister Pickering continued. "A black woman went to the Davis Plantation last night. The growers think she is a man but she is, in fact, a woman. She went to visit Delilah, the woman of whom you spoke. My friend has not yet returned. Doctor Ross, would you be so kind as to visit the slave quarters and ask whether a visitor went there last night?"

The Birdman asked, "What is the woman's name?"

Mister Pickering hesitated before he said, "They call her Moses."

The doctor said, "I understand your need for caution for I have heard of Harriet Tubman, the woman they call Moses. She is well known among the slaves as a brave woman who leads runaways to freedom. But among the white growers, she is known as a man who encourages slaves to run away. I think there are parts of your story that you are not telling me, but I understand that with the lives of others in your hands you cannot be too careful. I'll go back to the Davis Plantation and try to find out what has happened to Moses. I'll be back in the morning."

The Birdman set off, his owl hoots fading as he walked away. I was thankful that Mister Pickering had not told him that we were hiding in the coffins, but he had told the stranger about Moses. What if the Birdman told Grower Davis that she was on his plantation?

That night we decided to stay in the coffins, ready to drive off if patrollers came. Mister Pickering said he would watch over us as we slept, and I prayed that he could keep us safe. I missed Moses. It was a very long night.

I woke up when I heard a bird call, the call of an owl. The Birdman greeted Mister Pickering and said, "Friend, both Moses and Delilah are safe, but they are trapped on Ghost Island. Moses made a raft and made her way to the island, but on the way back, the raft fell apart and Moses and Delilah nearly drowned. With some difficulty, they were able to get back to the island but there are no trees there and no wood to make another raft. Grower Davis keeps a rowboat locked on the shore and I have asked for the key. He thinks I will be searching for owls along the river tonight but, instead, I will be rescuing Moses and Delilah."

Mister Pickering's tone was serious. "Doctor Ross, it is one thing to give coins and maps to slaves, but it is another to assist Moses in leading runaways to freedom. If you are caught, you will face a heavy fine or a long jail sentence."

"I thank you for your words of warning," the doctor said. "But I will be honoured to help Moses; I welcome the opportunity to act on my beliefs. Now, there is nothing to be done before nightfall except eat and rest. I have brought you food, thinking you must be hungry."

Mister Pickering said, "You are kind to bring food . . . and food aplenty."

The Birdman laughed. "I thought some of the dead might be hungry, too. Am I right in thinking there are runaways in those coffins?"

Mister Pickering called softly, "Obadiah, Deborah, Josiah and Rebecca, you can show yourselves." One by one, we opened the coffins and climbed down from the wagon.

As the Birdman shook hands with each of us, I saw that his face was kind and etched with the lines that come from laughter.

After the Birdman passed us thick slices of ham and bread, he said gently, "Please be ready to move around midnight. You will have to make room on this hearse for me. After this, my welcome on the plantation will be over."

With that he turned and disappeared into the thick forest. After a while, his bird calls faded into the distance.

We waited for nightfall, then waited still longer. Our safety now depended upon the Birdman, a stranger we had just met. The Birdman said he was willing to help us, but was he as clever as Moses? Would he be able to convince Grower Davis that he was looking for owls along the river?

I looked up at the sky and saw stars overhead. I heard leaves rustling in the wind, frogs croaking and mosquitoes swarming. I strained to hear the sound of an owl call but the Birdman was not yet coming.

CHAPTER SEVEN

Delilah

LATER THAT NIGHT, I heard a rustling in the woods, then three hoots of an owl. The Birdman! My heart was racing as I saw three figures running through the woods. I ran to Moses and wrapped my arms around her. "Moses, Moses, I was so worried about you."

Moses grinned and gave me a big hug. Then she took my hand and pulled me toward the hearse. "Come on, child, your Moses is here. Now we have to put some distance between us and Grower Davis. Delilah will ride up front but the rest of us need to get back in our coffins. I'll tell you about my adventures later."

Delilah climbed up to the driver's seat and sat down between Mister Pickering and the Birdman. Then the rest of us climbed into our coffins. Mister Pickering set the horses off at a fast pace. When would Grower Davis discover that Delilah was gone from the island? And what would he think when he learned that the Birdman had left in the middle of the night?

After we had travelled many miles, Mister Pickering pulled the hearse into a clearing and told us we could come out of our coffins. Moses laughed, "Mercy, those horses must be tired—almost as tired as I am. We have covered some distance this night. Now it's time for me to introduce Delilah properly."

I stared at Delilah. Not only was her skin white, but her hair was straight. I looked closely at her eyes and saw that they were dark brown. Delilah smiled shyly. "I'm glad to be travelling with you. Since I put out word on the grapevine that I was ready to ride the Underground Railroad, I have been waiting for Moses to come. It was a surprise when she found me on Ghost Island."

Moses laughed, "And even more of a surprise when the raft sank and we almost drowned. Then the Birdman came and surprised the both of us."

Moses took my face in her hands. "You were worried about Moses, weren't you, child?"

"Yes, Moses, I was." It was hard to remember that, at one time, I had been afraid of Moses because now she was like another mother to me.

Moses put one arm around me and the other around Delilah. "Delilah, this is Rebecca and her father Obadiah and her mother Deborah. This is her uncle Josiah and this is Mister Pickering, a conductor on the Underground Railroad. Mister Pickering has kindly brought us all the way from North Carolina and will drive us the rest of the way to the steamboat."

Delilah smiled at each of us and said, "I'm sorry you'll have to pretend to be my slaves on the steamboat, but Moses tells me that it's the safest way for us to travel up the river to St. Louis."

Uncle Josiah said, "It'll be no trouble. We all have plenty of practice being slaves . . . You sure are pretty."

Delilah laughed and Uncle Josiah laughed, too. Then Mister Pickering climbed back onto the hearse with Delilah and the Birdman, and said, "Now it's time for us to move on again as we have many miles to go before we get to Memphis. This state of Tennessee is a dangerous place for runaways, so hide in your coffins and don't open them until I give the word."

After travelling for three days, we reached the outskirts of Memphis. That night we slept in the woods. In the morning, we climbed back into the coffins and Mister Pickering drove the hearse into the town itself. I wished that I could sit on the driver's seat with Delilah, the Birdman and Mr. Pickering because I had never seen a city, but I had to be content with the sounds and smells. I heard men calling to one another and wagons rattling down the streets. The smell of bacon and coffee made my stomach grumble.

At last we stopped and Mister Pickering quietly told us, "We should give thanks to God, for we have reached Memphis." We opened the coffins and saw that he had driven the hearse into an empty carriage house. An old man in a black suit stood waiting for us, and Mister Pickering shook his hand before introducing us. "My brethren and sisters, this is Caleb, a Friend who lives in Memphis. Caleb will drive you in his carriage to the steamboat landing. He will give you money for your passage and a trunk with fancy hats and dresses for you, Delilah. The Birdman will say he is your brother and the two of you will board the steamboat first. The Birdman will pay for your passage and two staterooms. It is likely that the ticket master will ask you for papers proving that you own the slaves and promise to return them to the South. There are forged papers in this handbag." He pulled a bag from the carriage and passed it to Delilah.

Pretending to be a slave would not be hard for us because we had always been slaves. But it would be hard for Delilah to act like a free woman. I was worried that the ticket master would know that Delilah was a slave. Moses seemed to understand as she said, "Don't worry, child. All black people look like slaves to white people and all fair-skinned people look free to them."

Mister Pickering said, "It is time for me to say goodbye." He paused and his face looked tired and sad. "I will miss you, I will truly miss you. My wife and I will pray that you reach Canada and live in freedom. And we will continue to pray that slavery is abolished before the end of our days." As he spoke, tears came to Mister Pickering's eyes.

I mumbled my thanks to this kind man. I could not speak easily for the lump in my throat. I had never before been so grateful for a white man's kindness.

After Mister Pickering left with the empty hearse, my pa said softly, "Rebecca, we must never forget that good man." I had never heard my pa call a white man a good man.

Caleb climbed onto the driver's seat of the carriage.

Delilah stepped into a corner of the carriage house and slipped into a pretty green dress. She looked like a beautiful white woman as she and the Birdman climbed into the back of the carriage. The rest of us walked behind, shuffling our feet and walking with our backs bent.

The road we followed ran beside the Mississippi River. From time to time, I lifted my head and took quick glances at the mighty river. It was so wide that I could scarcely see the far bank. Along the shore, men were loading and unloading crates and barrels from boats. Mules pulled barges full of grain. Steamboats paddled their way up and down the river, and there was hustle and bustle everywhere.

Caleb stopped the carriage at the steamboat landing and walked to the back of the carriage. He spoke to us in a whisper, "Alas, from now on, I must be harsh with you, so people believe you are slaves."

The Birdman took Delilah's hand and helped her out of the carriage. Arm in arm, they walked up the gangplank to the boat. Gruffly, Caleb shouted at Uncle Josiah, "Get over here, boy. Pick up this trunk and carry it onto that steamboat." Then Caleb shoved my pa. "Carry these bags onto the boat." My pa picked up two bags, one in each hand, and shuffled up the gangplank. We all kept our faces down, hoping to be invisible to the captain and crew.

A deckhand yelled at my uncle. "You, put that trunk on the deck. Then move aside." I stayed close to Moses; we were out in the open, without a safe place to hide if something went wrong. I watched fearfully as the Birdman and Delilah walked up to the ticket master.

The Birdman said, "My sister, Miss Ross, and I wish to pay for passage and two staterooms. My sister has brought her slaves with her, for she will be staying in St. Louis for several months, caring for our mother who is gravely ill."

The ticket master took the money from the Birdman's hand without a pause. "Sir, here are your tickets. You and the lady can go to your staterooms. One of my men will show your slaves where to carry the trunk and bags, then we'll take your slaves to the hold below. Do you think they'll cause trouble? If so, we can chain them to posts in the slave pen."

"No, there will be no need to do that," said the Birdman. "These slaves will cause no trouble."

A steward walked up to the Birdman and said, "Excuse me, Sir. I assume you are the owner of the slaves?"

The Birdman shook his head. "No, they belong to my

sister, Miss Ross. She has the deeds of ownership in her handbag."

The steward looked at Delilah. I could see that her hands shook as she opened her bag and passed the forged papers to the man. He looked at them quickly and said, "Thank you, Miss Ross, that's fine. Now please sign this affidavit that you will return your slaves to the South." Delilah looked at the Birdman and her eyes were wide with fear. She did not know how to read nor write.

The Birdman quickly came to her rescue and said to the steward, "Sir, my poor sister is not used to signing papers. I'm afraid she leads a sheltered life on the plantation as our father manages all of the family's business. Please permit me to sign the affidavit for her."

He pulled a roll of bills from his pocket and passed it to the steward. "For your understanding, Sir, a little extra . . ."

The steward smiled and said, "Welcome aboard!"

I glanced at Moses and ventured a small smile. We had succeeded.

CHAPTER EIGHT

The Steamboat

AFTER MY PA AND UNCLE JOSIAH carried the trunk and bags to the staterooms, a deckhand shoved us down steep stairs and pushed us into a pen. He locked a heavy wooden door behind us. The pen was full of slaves, and many of the men were chained to posts. I gagged at the stench of hot, crowded bodies.

The heat was stifling. A boiler sat above a huge fire that burned in a metal box. An overseer yelled at the slaves, ordering them to throw more logs onto the fire. An old woman saw that I was frightened and explained that the fire made steam to turn the paddlewheel. "That's why it's called a steamboat," she said. "The steam rising out of the boiler turns the paddlewheel at the back of the boat. We'll be hot all the way to St. Louis."

Moses said to us, "Find yourselves a seat because we're going to be here for some time." Then Moses put her arm around my shoulders and whispered, "Honey, I've been in worse places, but it sure is hot down here!"

That night a deckhand came down to the pen and shouted, "Who's Rebecca? Miss Ross, she wants Rebecca to take care of her. Hurry up, girl, don't waste my time."

I looked at Moses who smiled and nodded her head. Then I understood that Delilah was helping me. I was scared to leave my family, but I had to obey; I had to obey because I was living as a slave again. The deckhand dragged me out of the pen, locked the door and took me to Delilah's stateroom. When he knocked on the door, Delilah opened it and waved me inside, shouting, "You lazy girl, you! Who was going to take care of me while you sat down below? There's work to be done." She thanked the deckhand and closed the door.

Delilah put her arms around me and whispered, "I'm sorry. I had to pretend to be your mistress. I figured the stateroom would be much nicer for you than the slave pen. Am I right?"

I nodded. "Yes, much nicer. I wish my family and

Moses weren't in that pen." Tears came to my eyes.

Delilah pointed to a small, round window. "Look, Rebecca, look out the porthole. See that steamboat passing by? That must be what our boat looks like." Lanterns lit the windows of the passing steamboat. At the back, sparks flew up from a smokestack and a wooden paddle-wheel churned through the water.

I looked around the stateroom itself. The room was like nothing I had ever seen before. It was much fancier than any room at Grower Brown's with a mirror set in a gold frame, wallpaper printed with pink roses and a bed heaped high with pillows and blankets.

Delilah invited me to sit down beside her on a small settee. "How old are you, Rebecca?"

"I'm twelve."

Delilah smiled. "How old do you think I am?"

I looked at her. "You're a woman."

There seemed to be sadness in her voice as Delilah said, "Yes, I'm eighteen. It was time for me to run away because the master was looking at me in a bad way."

I knew that the growers favoured pretty slave girls, and Delilah was more than pretty, she was beautiful. She looked at me and frowned. "Now, if you're going to pretend to be my stateroom slave and walk out on the deck behind the Birdman and me, you have to have a bath. Right now you're filthy from all that time in the coffin, but we'll get you clean. First, you'll have to get pails of hot water from the kitchen."

I walked along the deck with an empty pail in each hand. The steamboat blew its whistle, and I jumped with fright. We were passing another boat, a boat going down the river to Memphis. I wondered whether there were slaves on that boat. Were they stoking a fire to make the paddlewheel turn, just like the slaves on our boat?

I found the kitchen but waited outside, jumping out of the way as the doors swung open and shut. I was scared to go in. Men in white shirts and white pants came in and out, carrying trays full of food. Then I got a glimpse of the cook, a woman who looked like Ada. I pushed the door open and walked in. The cook was stirring huge pots of food, but when she saw the pails I was carrying, she said, "Child, come to the stove and I'll give you hot water for your missus."

She poured steaming water into the pails and I thanked her. I tried to carry the pails so their heat didn't burn my legs as I hurried back to the stateroom. When I knocked on the door, Delilah quickly opened it. "Rebecca, you took so long, I was scared." She took the heavy pails and poured the water into a metal tub.

"I'll get into the bath first," Delilah said. "I'm dirty but not as dirty as you!"

Delilah lowered herself into the hot water and bathed quickly. When she stepped out of the bath, she said, "Now it's your turn, Rebecca. The water is still warm." She poured water over me and rubbed soap into my hair. When we were through, Delilah chose a lavender-coloured dress for herself and a simple brown dress for me, a plain dress a slave would wear. My dress was too big but Delilah tied a scarf around my waist to hold it up.

The Birdman knocked on the door and came in, carrying a plate of food for Delilah. "Rebecca, what are you doing here?"

Then Delilah laughed and said, "Well, a fine lady like me needs a slave girl to look after her, that's how she got here."

"That was a clever idea!" the Birdman said.

Delilah and I shared the fried chicken, okra and sweet potato pie, but I thought about my family and felt sad. They would not be eating like this. I looked out the window and saw the lights of other boats passing us on the river. The floor of the stateroom shook gently as the giant paddlewheel kept turning. I was a long way from Grower Brown's plantation.

I asked the Birdman, "Will you take us out on the deck? I'll walk behind you and Delilah and pretend to be her servant." I wanted to walk on the deck, for no matter what happened, I knew I would never forget this night on the steamboat.

He smiled. "Yes, let's all go out. It's a fine night."

Delilah found two shawls and put one over my shoulders. The night air was cool as we stepped onto the deck. There were bright stars in the sky and the Birdman pointed to the Big Dipper. I smiled, knowing that the North Star led to freedom; it seemed closer than it had been at the plantation.

As we walked to the front of the steamboat, we saw a man holding an enormous wooden wheel, with spokes like a wagon wheel. The Birdman said, "That's the pilot. He stands on that raised platform, called the bridge, and steers, finding safe passage along the river." Every few minutes, we heard the pilot call out, "Depth?" Another man stood on the deck below and took soundings with a long pole that measured the depth of the water. He shouted to the pilot, "Mark Twain." The Birdman explained that sandbars were continually shifting from place to place in the Mississippi River. The boat needed to stay in deep water or it would run aground. "Mark Twain" meant two fathoms or twelve feet.

Another steamboat passed by. Sparks flew up from its smokestack and fell like rain on the river. Then the boat went around a bend and disappeared from sight. I thought of my family down below deck. I remembered the heat and the smell of that pen, and, despite the beauty of the river passage, I hoped it would end quickly.

We stayed on the deck for a long time. In the darkness, the fact that the Birdman and Delilah had white skin and I had black skin did not seem to make any difference. The Birdman walked us back to Delilah's room and Delilah made a bed for me on the floor. I lay down on the soft blankets, resting my head on a feather pillow, and fell asleep thinking of the North Star.

When I woke up, the sun was shining through the small round window. Delilah was still sleeping so I stayed quiet and still until she awakened. That morning she put on a clean blue-coloured dress with white lace at the collar. I wore the same brown dress because a slave girl would have only one dress.

The Birdman knocked on the door and said, "I think it is safer for you to stay in the stateroom during the day,

Delilah. There is no need for you to go on deck where other passengers, especially men, will want to make your acquaintance. Rebecca can bring you breakfast on a tray and you two can share the food."

I asked the Birdman if I could go to see my family and Moses, but he shook his head sadly. "No, that would put all of you at risk. I'm sorry, Rebecca."

The Birdman and I walked to the upper deck to get breakfast for Delilah. As we neared the dining room, I saw a man sitting beside a pretty white woman, talking and laughing. My heart stopped, and for a moment, I could not breathe.

I quickly turned my back to the man and woman and whispered to the Birdman, "It is Grower Brown's son— Master Jeff—sitting on the deck."

The Birdman was shocked. "Oh, no. Are you sure, Rebecca?"

I nodded. There was no doubt that I had seen Master Jeff. I kept my face down as I followed the Birdman back to Delilah's stateroom. When we walked into the room, Delilah could see the fear on our faces. She asked, "What is it? What happened?"

"Rebecca saw Master Jeff, the son of the man who was her master, sitting on deck," the Birdman said. "She is sure it is him. This was not what we planned, no, not at all. This is a very unwelcome complication."

Delilah saw that I was trembling and took my hand in hers. I looked at her and said, "When I saw Master Jeff, I realized that our journey has not taken us very far from slavery."

CHAPTER NINE

Disaster on Board

❧

THE BIRDMAN SAT in the stateroom, his forehead deeply furrowed. "Rebecca and Delilah, you should not go out on the deck again. If anyone asks, I will say you both fell ill. Fortunately, Rebecca's family and Moses are out of sight. I must warn them that Jeff is on the boat before we disembark in St. Louis. That's when there's a danger that he will see them. I wonder why on earth Master Jeff is here? Why is he going north?"

I remembered the meeting Grower Brown and Master Jeff had called, when all the growers in the county had come to the plantation, and Master Jeff had told them about the Knights of the Golden Circle. I looked at the Birdman. "I know why he is going north."

The Birdman was surprised. "Please tell us what you know, Rebecca. This is very important."

I said, "Just before we ran away, Master Jeff and the other growers formed a secret group. They called it a castle, part of the Knights of the Golden Circle. Master Jeff said he would go to Cincinnati to meet the leader of the Knights. He planned to take him money, money to hire more bounty hunters."

The Birdman was silent, thinking about what I had said. "But why is he going to St. Louis then? Cincinnati is to the east."

I shook my head. I could not answer that.

"I'll go back on deck," the Birdman said. "I'll find a way to talk with Jeff and find out why he's here."

I said, "Master Jeff likes to play poker. Do you know how to play poker?"

The Birdman laughed. "Not well. I'll pretend to be a wealthy gentleman who always loses. Then I can be sure that Jeff will want to play poker with me."

As he left, the Birdman locked the door. Delilah slumped in her chair and tears rolled down her cheeks.

Even though I was afraid, I said to Delilah, "Have faith. We're going to reach Canada."

We waited a long time for the Birdman to come back. Finally, we heard a key turning in the lock, and the Birdman came in and told us what he had learned. "I sat down beside Jeff and we started talking. He told me about your family running away, led by a man named Moses. As you know, the growers believe that Moses is a man. Jeff said he thought the Quakers were hiding you runaways, Quakers or some other abolitionists. He told me he had travelled from town to town hiring patrollers, and along the way, he met Quakers who told him slavery is evil. Jeff thinks Quakers hold that view because they own small farms, not big plantations. He believes slaves are necessary if you want to make money on a plantation.

"I asked Jeff where he's going. He said he's going first to St. Louis, then on to Cincinnati. When I asked him why, he told me about the Knights of the Golden Circle. He is very proud of the fact that he formed a castle in South Carolina. Just as you said, Rebecca, he's taking money to the founder of the Knights to hire more bounty hunters. On the way he's stopping in St. Louis to see the trial of a slave named Dred Scott. The case will decide whether slaves are free under the law if they live for some time in a free state but are forced to go back to a slave state. The key issue is whether any black man, free or slave, can claim citizenship in this country. The trial will have profound implications."

The Birdman continued, "Now it seems I have become a spy, as well as a doctor and an ornithologist! For the rest of our time on the river, I will keep company with Jeff, unpleasant as he is, so I can learn more about his plans. People say it's important to keep your enemies close to you."

The Birdman left us in the stateroom. Later he told us how he warned Moses and my family. He began by telling a deckhand that his sister's slaves had stolen a necklace and he needed to go down to the slave pen. In the hold, the Birdman pretended to be angry, shouting at Moses and my ma, "Come close so I can look in your eyes and see who is the thief." When they were close to him, he whispered, "Grower Brown's son, Jeff, is on this boat. When we reach St. Louis, you must be careful not to be seen by him."

Moses gasped, "Has he seen Rebecca?"

The Birdman said, "No, and she is staying out of sight."

Moses said, "You will have to distract him when it's time to get off the boat."

Every evening, the Birdman went to the salon and played cards with Master Jeff. The Birdman said a young slave called Boots served them whiskey and lit their cigars. Because his master, Wyatt, was most particular about his boots, the young slave had to polish them morning, noon and night. The Birdman said Wyatt was as nasty as Jeff.

Master Jeff confided in the Birdman, telling him that he was gambling with the money the growers had given him for the Knights of the Golden Circle. Jeff had lost a considerable amount of money but he was sure he would win it back, and more besides. The Birdman pretended to sympathize with Master Jeff over his losses. In order to win Jeff's trust, the Birdman said he was furious that the federal marshals weren't capturing runaways and that Jeff and the other growers had to spend their own money to hire patrollers.

Master Jeff said, "What about hiring patrollers in Canada? They could catch runaway slaves there, just as they do in the United States." My heart sank when the Birdman told us what Jeff had said. Would patrollers continue to hunt us down in Canada?

The next night brought a disaster that changed our lives. Only later did we learn what happened on deck. When the last poker hand had been played, the Birdman walked out on the deck and saw Boots standing near the pilot house. The pilot shouted to the Birdman, "We are on the Missouri side of the river now. After two more bends, we'll see the lights of St. Louis." He raised a telescope to his eye and searched the river for sandbars. Suddenly he shouted, "Hard to starboard! Hard to starboard!" The boat turned, very slowly, then shuddered and stopped.

The Birdman told us that he was thrown forward and fell on the deck. As he rose to his feet, there was a loud explosion. He looked over the side of the boat and saw flames. He shouted to Boots, "Run to the slave pen and get those people out!" Then the Birdman hurried to the stateroom to save Delilah and me.

We were frightened when the boat shuddered to a stop but relieved when the Birdman threw open our door and shouted, "We have hit a sandbar and the steamboat is sinking. We have to get off the boat quickly!"

"What about my family and Moses? They're trapped below," I cried out.

"I've sent Boots to free them," he told me. "There's no time to waste. You and Delilah must get off the boat now. In the confusion, it's not likely that Jeff will see you, Rebecca, but you must cover your face, just in case."

Delilah and I ran onto the deck with the Birdman.

People were screaming and running in all directions. Delilah was knocked down but we helped her to her feet. The Birdman pushed through the crowd of panicked people. When we got to the side of the boat, he said, "I'm going down below to help the others. We'll meet on the sandbar. Now, jump!" Delilah and I jumped and landed in shallow water. We were safe, but that was little comfort as I thought about my family and Moses trapped below.

When the Birdman ran below, he did not see any white overseers. They had run up on deck to save themselves, leaving the slaves trapped in the pen. Boots was trying to break the heavy lock on the wooden door but the lock was too strong. My pa covered his face with his shirt and ran into the flames. My ma screamed, "Obadiah, what are you doing?"

My pa grabbed an iron poker the slaves had used to push logs into the fire box and raced back to the other side of the pen. He raised the poker and slammed it into the wooden door, splintering the wood. Then Uncle Josiah took the poker and freed the slaves who were chained to posts. At last, all the slaves were able to run up to the deck and the Birdman rushed up the steps behind them.

The Birdman pushed through the crowd of frightened

passengers and led my family and Moses to the side of the boat. I heard the Birdman shout, "Jump!"

I saw my pa and ma hesitate. They were deathly afraid of water and were too frightened to jump. Uncle Josiah grabbed a long pole the deckhands had used to measure the river's depth and pushed it into the water. "It's only knee-deep!" he shouted. Then Uncle Josiah and my folks jumped from the burning boat, followed by Moses and the Birdman.

We gathered on the sandbar and ran to the shore. The Birdman shouted, "Keep moving! That boiler could explode and release a cloud of steam."

We climbed onto the riverbank, grateful to be alive. Moses said, "Friends, we're on the Missouri side of the river and Missouri is a slave state. We need to get across to the Illinois side as quickly as we can."

As the fire spread through the wooden frame of the boat, sparks fell on our skin, burning our faces and arms. Passengers and slaves who were trapped on the boat screamed. Some jumped to the safety of the sandbar, but others jumped off the far side of the boat, where the water ran deep and the current was strong.

CHAPTER TEN

Saving an Enemy

WE STARED AT THE burning steamboat. All of a sudden, I gasped, "I see Master Jeff! I see him in the water." In the light cast by the fire, I saw him floating in the river. His arms rested on a wooden plank and he seemed lifeless.

I hesitated for a moment. Master Jeff was hateful but he was Miss Clarissa's brother and I knew she loved some part of him. Suddenly, I knew I could not leave him in the river. I grabbed the pole Uncle Josiah had carried from the boat and plunged into the river. Holding the pole with one hand, I reached back with the other and asked my pa to hold tight. My pa held on to Uncle Josiah and he held on to the Birdman, making a chain of people, our hands holding tight to one another. I sank deeper and deeper into the black water of the river. I did not know how to swim but I knew I had to save Master Jeff.

I stretched as far as I could into the current, working the end of the pole under Master Jeff's body. I pulled him closer until I could grab his arm. "I've got him!" I shouted. The others pulled and pulled until we were able to drag him onto the sandbar. Then Uncle Josiah and the Birdman carried Master Jeff onto shore.

Master Jeff was so limp that I thought he was dead. The Birdman shouted, "Help me turn him over so I can get the water out of his lungs."

I remembered then that the Birdman was a doctor and knew how to heal people. He pumped Master Jeff's back and water poured out of his mouth. The Birdman put two fingers on his neck and said, "He is alive, but barely so."

My pa said, "You did the right thing, Rebecca, by saving Master Jeff. On the plantation, I saw some slaves turn as mean as their growers. I'm glad that didn't happen to you."

Master Jeff opened his eyes and stared at my pa. He croaked, "Obadiah!"

The Birdman said, "Jeff, this man and his daughter saved your life." Jeff shook his head in disbelief. We stepped back into the shadows.

The Birdman took Moses aside. "If we leave Master Jeff here, alone, he may die; but if you stay with him, you'll lose your freedom. You must move deep into the woods while I stay here. As a doctor, it's my duty to care for him."

Moses answered in a low voice. "Yes, you should stay with him until a boat comes and takes him to St. Louis. But as soon as you can, you must get to Alton, on the Illinois side of the river. Find Priscilla Baltimore, a freed slave, and ask her to send boats to carry us to Illinois. We'll wait in the woods until we hear your owl hoots."

The Birdman nodded. "I'll find Priscilla and come back with boats."

Moses said, "Thank God for you. Now be gone. Tell Priscilla to bring me a gun. My revolver is dripping wet and it may be no good."

The Birdman went back to Master Jeff and knelt beside him. I saw moving lanterns on the river and realized that boats were coming to the rescue. I knew then that Master Jeff would be saved. Then we left the riverbank and Moses said, "We're going to move deep into the woods before we settle down for the night. Missouri is a mean state if you're black and even meaner if you're a runaway."

My ma said, "Moses, what will happen next? How will we get across the river if the Birdman doesn't get boats?"

Moses looked at my ma. "I'm not going to lie to you, Deborah. We're in a tight spot, a spot we didn't plan to be in. Getting off the boat in St. Louis would have been risky, but not as risky as our current situation. But the Birdman is a good man and a clever one. He saved me and Delilah once; he will save us again. I know he will get boats."

My ma said, "It's still hard for me to believe that there are white people like the Birdman who are willing to risk their lives to help us."

Moses nodded. "Yes, white people come in different kinds, good and bad. Some help us and others believe we should live in bondage." Then Moses laughed. "I can hardly talk with all the smoke and ashes in my throat. Let's get some water and wash out our mouths. A little ways back, we passed a creek."

When we found the creek, we sat on the ground and splashed water on our faces. We drank our fill but had nothing to eat.

Uncle Josiah said, "Obadiah, remember when we were

young? Sometimes we had to go for days without a meal. I guess we can do it again."

My pa nodded. "Yes, I guess we can. Maybe if we don't think about our empty bellies, it'll be easier. Moses, will you tell us about Illinois? What's it like for black people in a free state?"

Moses leaned her back against a tree and started talking. "When we get to Illinois, we're going to stay in the Freedom Village of Brooklyn, a village near Alton. Twenty-five years ago Priscilla Baltimore gathered eleven black families and together they founded the first black town in America. Soon you'll meet Priscilla. She is a strong woman, a very strong woman."

"Like you," I said.

"No, child, she is much stronger. I am weak beside her."

Uncle Josiah said, "Then she must be a powerful woman, Moses, because you are stronger than anybody I know, man or woman."

My ma sat up. "Moses, can we settle in Freedom Village? I am tired of running and hiding, of being frightened day in and day out."

Delilah said, "Yes, I'd like to stay in Freedom Village, too."

Moses looked at my ma and Delilah. "I know it's hard being on the run but you can't stay in Freedom Village. You're runaways. Even in Illinois, a free state, there will be bounty hunters looking for you. Priscilla is a freed black so she's safe."

My ma sighed. "The Lord knows I wish I could stop. I feel weary enough to be an old woman. Obadiah is strong and he could work on a farm in Freedom Village. I could work on a farm, too, and Rebecca could help a white woman, cooking and cleaning."

I stood in front of my ma and said, "No, I want to live in freedom. I am travelling from midnight to dawn and I won't stop until I see the sunrise."

Moses said, "You are some girl, Rebecca. I've led many children to freedom. Most of them cry and whine all the way to Canada. But not you. You have a hunger for freedom as strong as any grown-up."

Uncle Josiah asked, "How can they call Illinois a free state when runaways can't settle there?"

Moses answered, "In Illinois, slavery was abolished thirty years ago but a lot of people don't want black folks to live there, whether they're slaves or freed blacks. Some years ago they made a law called the Black Codes of 1819. Any slave who wants to become a freed black has to register at the county courthouse and pay his white owner to become free. I don't think Grower Brown or Grower Davis will let you buy your freedom, do you?"

Delilah and my ma shook their heads. My ma said, "No, they wouldn't want to see us set free, no matter how much money we gave them."

My pa was puzzled. "How did the blacks in Freedom Village get to be free? How did they get the money?"

Moses answered. "Priscilla's master was also her father. He was a minister in Kentucky but he didn't always follow the Lord's teachings. Maybe he didn't like looking at Priscilla and knowing she was his daughter so he sold her to another minister, a reverend in St. Louis. The new master made her work all day for him, but in the evenings, he let her earn money for herself. She sewed dresses for the white women in town, and over the years, she saved five hundred dollars, enough to buy her freedom."

My pa shook his head. "Five hundred dollars! That's a lot of money."

Uncle Josiah said, "Yes, it's a lot of money but now she's free. What's it like to live as a freed slave in Freedom Village?"

Moses said, "The people in Freedom Village are free

but only in some ways. Under the law, they are free but there is always fear, fear in the hearts of the white people and fear in the hearts of the black people."

I asked, "What about Canada? What will it be like to live in Canada?"

Moses said, "I live in a place called St. Catharines in Canada. Near my town, there's a big river that divides the United States and Canada. The river goes over a mighty waterfall—Niagara Falls. The roar of that waterfall tells everybody that there's a border there. And that border means everything to black people. In both countries, there are people who hold black people apart, but in Canada the law says there shall be no slavery. At one time, there was slavery in Canada and fear and hatred remain. The law can't change that in our lifetime, but the law can protect you so you are never forced back into bondage."

We nestled into the fallen leaves on the ground. I lay awake during that chilly night, thinking about freedom. I had been born a slave and I knew what it meant to be a slave. Now I was a runaway, no longer answering to Grower Brown. What would it be like to be free? What lay ahead?

CHAPTER ELEVEN

Underground Ferry
to Freedom

WE WOKE UP EARLY THE next morning, hungry and thirsty. Moses told us to stay in the woods while she and Delilah walked back to where the steamboat had run aground. Smoke hung in the air over the charred remains of the steamboat. Even though they were alone on the shore, Delilah was afraid to walk out in the open. But when Moses reminded Delilah that she was safe with her white skin, she walked out on the sandbar, looking for any food that might have been cast from the boat. When she found nothing she hurried back to Moses, and they returned empty-handed to where we had stayed in the woods.

We were all hungry. Uncle Josiah said, "I bet there are some hickory trees in these woods. We can eat those nuts. They won't fill us up but they'll keep us from starving." He headed off in the direction of the river and soon came back with hickory nuts wrapped in his shirt. He picked up a rock and cracked one of the nuts, then gave the nutmeat to Delilah. She smiled and broke the piece in two. With her small hand, she fed a half to my uncle. We broke open the rest of the nuts, chewing each one carefully.

We waited for the Birdman to return. That night, we listened for his bird calls but they did not come. On the second evening, Moses told us to wait deep in the woods while she went to the river to look for the Birdman. Whenever Moses left us, our spirits sank and we worried about what would happen next. What if the Birdman had been arrested for helping us runaways?

Then I heard a wonderful sound, a sound that filled me with hope. It was the Birdman's owl hoots. I ran through the woods to meet Moses and the Birdman.

Moses said, "The Underground Ferry has arrived with

boats. Come quick. We have only a few more hours of darkness and we must cross the river before daylight."

At the river's edge, I saw three boats. A man motioned for me, my pa and my ma to get into the closest one. A black woman held the oars. She said softly, "The Underground Ferry has come for you." The man pushed the boat off the shore, jumped in and sat beside the woman. They each took an oar and started to row.

My pa said, "Here, let me help." But the woman shook her head. "No, I will row. You just sit down. You've been running and hiding; you must be tired."

The woman said, "My name is Priscilla—Priscilla Baltimore. We're taking you across the river to Illinois. You'll be safer there than you were in Missouri, but still, Illinois is a dangerous place for you. We have a wagon waiting to take you to our town, Freedom Village, where you can hide." Both the man and the woman had revolvers in their belts, and the man had a rifle slung over his shoulder.

The oars splashed noisily in the river, and I worried that the bounty hunters would hear us. Looking up at the sky, I feared the coming of dawn. Priscilla seemed to sense my fear. "Don't worry, child. We'll be on the Illinois side well before sunrise."

When we reached the far shore, we pulled the boats up on the riverbank. Priscilla said, "Follow me. The wagon is waiting up ahead. We have food for you. I'm sure you are hungry!"

Uncle Josiah said, "Hungry for food and hungry for freedom!"

We walked one by one behind Priscilla until we saw a big covered wagon. A black man smiled at us and passed us cornbread, bacon and boiled eggs. Then he handed us jugs of cool, clean water. After we climbed into the wagon and headed north to Freedom Village, the Birdman told us what had happened in St. Louis. "The night the steamboat burned, I stayed with Jeff. His mind was confused. At times, he thought that I was the one who had saved him. I said nothing, for I didn't want him to remember that it was Rebecca who had saved him. But after a while, he remembered what had happened, and he said, 'My slaves, a man called Obadiah and his girl, Rebecca, they pulled me out of the river, didn't they? Why would those runaways save my life?'"

The Birdman went on, "Meanwhile, the captain took a count of passengers and slaves. Everyone was standing on the sandbar, the white passengers at one end and the slaves at the other. Deckhands stood guard over the slaves. When small boats arrived from St. Louis, some of the passengers wanted to take their slaves with them but the captain refused. He said the slaves could walk to St. Louis along the riverbank and his crew would make sure none ran away. The captain and I loaded Jeff onto one of the boats along with other injured passengers. From time to time, Jeff felt strong enough to talk, and he told me over and over again that Rebecca and Obadiah had saved his life. He couldn't understand why.

"He should have been grateful, but as Jeff grew stronger, he became more and more determined to catch you. When Jeff regained a bit of strength, he sent a message to the castle of the Knights of the Golden Circle in St. Louis and learned that the Grand Founder, George Bickley, had also come to St. Louis to see the Dred Scott trial."

Moses asked, "Did you meet Bickley?"

The Birdman nodded. "Yes, I did. George Bickley is a most unpleasant man. He walked into Jeff's hospital room and introduced himself as the Grand Founder of the Knights of the Golden Circle. Bickley kept pulling a gold watch out of his pocket, reminding me of Wyatt and the other gamblers on the steamboat. Bickley is as greasy as a side of bacon. Jeff gave him what money he had left after gambling and said the growers in South

Carolina raised the money to hire more bounty hunters. As soon as I could, I said goodbye and hurried to Alton."

Moses looked at the Birdman. "You look tired. I hope you know how grateful we are."

The Birdman smiled. "I am happy to play a small part in helping you to reach freedom. By the way, Bickley said most runaways cross the river from St. Louis to Alton, and from there, they ride the Chicago and Alton Railroad to Chicago."

Moses looked at Priscilla. "If Bickley thinks we're riding on the Chicago and Alton Railroad, we'll have to travel a different way."

The Birdman agreed. "When you leave, I will go to Philadelphia to meet William Still. I want to tell him what I learned about the Knights of the Golden Circle." He turned to me and explained, "William is the founder of the Philadelphia Vigilance Committee which passes important information to the conductors on the Underground Railroad."

I asked, "What does 'vigilance' mean?"

"Vigilance means keeping watch over you and keeping you safe."

I mumbled the word "vigilance" and hoped that Mister Still was watching over Moses, my family and me.

Priscilla said, "Can you see Freedom Village?" I looked down the road and saw the town with a few houses and a large church. Many people came out to greet us: men, women and children—all black.

They led us to the church. I pointed to a large sign above the door and asked Moses what it said. She laughed. "Child, I wish I could read, but I can't. When you get to Canada, you'll go to school. Then you can tell Moses what that sign says."

Priscilla heard my question. "That sign says 'Founded by Chance, Sustained by Courage.'"

Inside the church, platters of food were laid on a long table. I was so hungry that I ate and ate until my stomach hurt. Later Priscilla walked us to her house where her husband and their four children welcomed us. They led us to the attic and we slept on blankets on the floor.

My ma rested her head on her hands and said, "Oh, Obadiah, I am so tired. I don't know whether I can go on."

My pa said, "You will find the strength to go on, just as I found the strength to follow Moses. I was afraid of running away, but I was wrong to be afraid. People like Ezekiel and the Birdman, the Pickerings and Priscilla have given me courage. We'll rest and then we'll move on."

My ma said, "Every day, I ask myself, what's best for Rebecca?"

My pa looked at me. "Deborah, I know what's best for her and so do you. Rebecca's mind is set on reaching freedom. She is not the same child who lived in slavery on the plantation. None of us are the same. I am a different man since we crossed the Mason–Dixon Line from slavery to this free state of Illinois, and I can feel that change even now."

"What do you mean, Obadiah?" my ma asked.

"When we were at Grower Brown's, he and his men could come to our shack at any time and beat me. There was nothing I could do. Nothing!"

"But, Obadiah, if the bounty hunters catch you now, they'll beat you."

"Yes, the bounty hunters could catch me and they could beat me. But the people of Freedom Village would fight them and I would fight them. I would fight for freedom. That's something important, that's what's different. I'm never going back to slavery."

CHAPTER TWELVE

The Handcars

❦

I WAS AWAKENED by Priscilla's words of alarm. "Bad news, Moses! One of our conductors, Mr. Shadow, has seen many bounty hunters riding into Alton. They're stirring up the white people, telling them runaways should be sent back to the South. I fear that a mob may march on Freedom Village."

Moses said, "We need to get moving—fast."

Priscilla said, "Yes, you must be on your way tonight; a mob is a very ugly and dangerous threat."

Delilah asked anxiously, "How can we leave Freedom

Village with so many bounty hunters looking for us?"

Priscilla answered, "Alas, this is not the first time our town has been surrounded. Tonight six wagons will assemble outside the church. The six wagons will head in different directions. The bounty hunters will follow them. Then another wagon, with all of you hidden inside, will drive north."

"Who will drive us?" Moses asked.

"A black man named James Thomas. He'll drive you to the spur line of the railroad in Litchfield. He has arranged for two handcars to be left in a shed there. You will use the handcars to move north on the spur line, travelling by night and sleeping by day. Along the way, there will be families to hide you."

Moses said, "Deborah and Delilah, I know you are weary of travelling, but we need to move on tonight. Are you ready?"

My ma put her arm around me and said, "My daughter wants to go to school in Canada, so I'm ready."

Delilah nodded her head and said, "I'm ready, too." She smiled at Uncle Josiah.

It was time to say goodbye to our trusted friend, the Birdman, who was heading to Philadelphia. As my pa reached for the Birdman's hand, the Birdman put his arms around my pa's shoulders. They stood hugging for a long time.

The Birdman said, "This is not the end of our friendship; we will meet again in Canada as free men."

In Priscilla's kitchen, we gathered around the stove, warming ourselves as we waited for Mister Thomas. We heard a knock on the door and a big black man came into the house. Priscilla said, "This is James Thomas."

He smiled at all of us and said to Moses, "It is a privilege and an honour to help you—and your friends, too. Moses is a name that is much respected in Freedom Village." Then Mister Thomas explained his plan for the next leg of our journey. "I have chosen a safe, slow route to Chicago. Tonight we'll travel by wagon, stopping and resting in Litchfield. Then we'll take two handcars and travel at night along the spur line. Only one train a day runs on that line and it runs during the daylight hours."

Mister Thomas led us to the door. "Please follow me to the wagon. You'll have to lie down so I can cover you with sacks of chicken feed. I have to make sure nobody can see you."

The night air was cold and Mister Thomas gave each of us a thick coat, the cloth heavy and rough. Moses told us the coats were made of wool, from the fleece of sheep.

"In the North, you'll be wearing wool all winter or you'll freeze!"

Mister Thomas lifted me into the wagon with a chuckle. "Child, you weigh nothing. Did Priscilla forget to feed you?"

Mister Thomas drove and drove through the dark night until he stopped in a thick forest. As he tethered the horse, he said, "We'll stay here with William and Mary Dodge. They have helped many runaway slaves. Maybe Mary will have some extra food for you, child. If you don't eat more, you're likely to blow away in a snowstorm."

As dawn filled the sky with light, Mister and Missus Dodge hid us in the attic of their small home. We passed the day, impatient to be on our way. At last, night fell and Mister Thomas led us back to the spur line. And, just as he had promised, we found two handcars in the shed.

"Now I'll show you how to pump these cars," Mister Thomas said. "We're going to pump all the way to Joliet! It will take about a week if we're lucky. I'll work one car with Moses, and, Obadiah and Josiah, you'll work the other car."

We divided ourselves so I rode with Mister Thomas, Moses and my ma while Delilah rode on the other car with my pa and Uncle Josiah. The cars were so small there was no room to lie down. Fearing I would fall off, I leaned into my ma and held tight.

Mister Thomas said, "Let's go. You'll be surprised at how fast we can move. Keep your car close to mine so we can call to one another if need be. Everybody will take turns working the levers, everybody but you, Rebecca. You're too little for this work."

I said I wanted to help. Mister Thomas laughed, "You're helping just by being you. Child, you don't weigh more than a shadow and it'll be easy to drive you down the line."

As Mister Thomas had promised, we moved at a fast pace. There was no moonlight and we could not see the rails, but the wheels followed the tracks. As we rolled through the night, Mister Thomas was quiet; he never stopped watching and listening. He told us that a train sometimes broke down and had to run late on the spur line. Hardly ever, he said, but he needed to stay alert, just in case.

As the wind blew down the neck of my coat and up my sleeves, I tried to pull my coat tighter around me. Every time I breathed out, my breath made steam, something I had never seen before. Mister Thomas and my pa wrapped scraps of blanket around the levers so their hands wouldn't freeze on the cold metal.

Pa challenged Uncle Josiah. "Remember when we were kids? You were always telling me you were the strongest. Well, let's just see if you can keep up with me."

Their car sped along until Mister Thomas called to them. "Slow down. We need to stay together. Just pump your car nice and steady."

Moses laughed, "You two rascals! You're going to wear yourselves out before we even get started. It's a long way to Joliet so you better listen to Mister Thomas!"

After many hours on the handcars, Mister Thomas said, "The sun will soon be up and we'll need to stop. There are likely to be bounty hunters in the next town so we'll pull off on a siding before we reach Decatur."

I shivered with cold and fear. Would bounty hunters catch us? I looked at the sky. On the plantation, I had loved the colours of sunrise but the dawn now frightened me. Once the sun came up, we would no longer be invisible.

CHAPTER THIRTEEN

Delayed

❧

WE HID THE HANDCARS and followed Mister Thomas to the home of white abolitionists, Amos and Tabitha Stewart. They were very old but they climbed a ladder, leading us to a hidden room below the eaves.

My pa was restless as we waited for the day to pass. On the plantation he had walked with his head down, his back bent. Now he walked tall and proud. Uncle Josiah looked at him and said, "It's hard just waiting here, isn't it, brother? We're both happier when we're travelling."

My pa nodded. "Yes, I'm anxious for the night to come so we can get back on the handcars."

"I'll be ready to go tonight," my ma said. "But right now, I'm tired and I'm glad to rest. I try to take my mind off my weariness by imagining what life will be like in Canada."

Mister Thomas said, "I don't know about life in Canada, but I can tell you about my life as a freed slave in Illinois. Most of the time, my wife and I feel safe. Our children go to school, they're learning to read and write, but they don't have any white friends. Most of the white people—young and old—they hold us apart. And there are times when we do not feel safe. Sometimes the fear and anger gets so strong that the white people form a mob; then we're fearful.

"Twenty years ago, a white man named Elijah Parish Lovejoy had a printing press in Alton. He was an abolitionist and he printed articles about the evil of slavery. He was shot by a mob as he stood in front of that printing press. The people in that mob were his neighbours. A shooting like that makes it hard to forget that many white people don't want us to live among them."

When the sun had set, we said goodbye to the Stewarts and walked back to the handcars. Along the way, Delilah mumbled, "I'm cold. So cold. I want to go home. Please take me home." Uncle Josiah wrapped his arms around her and steadied her as she started coughing.

Moses said, "Rebecca, you stand by Delilah. If she coughs, hold a blanket to her mouth. We have to stay quiet."

We inched forward on the handcars until Mister Thomas motioned for us to stop. We looked ahead and saw lanterns in the distance. Mister Thomas whispered, "I think bounty hunters are watching the road up ahead. It runs beside the track for some distance. I'll go back to the Stewarts and ask Amos to find a way to lead those men away from the tracks."

We huddled together on the handcars. Delilah started to moan and Moses put a hand on her forehead. Frowning, she said, "Delilah has a fever. She's burning up."

We heard Mister Stewart riding fast in the distance. He rode to the bounty hunters and shouted, "Come quick. Runaways have stolen food from my kitchen." The bounty hunters picked up their lanterns and ran down the road.

Mister Thomas appeared out of the darkness and said, "Amos has led the men away. Now it's time to start pumping these cars and get past that checkpoint before they come back."

We hurried past the spot where we had seen the lanterns and kept pumping until we reached the town of Decatur. No lights burned in the houses and stores we passed, and I hoped that every person in that town was fast asleep. We glided quietly through the town and back into the country. I whispered to Delilah, "We made it through the town without being seen. We're invisible again." I don't know whether she heard my words or not. She moaned and closed her eyes.

Mister Thomas said, "We must get Delilah to a safe place. She needs a doctor."

Moses agreed. "Yes, she's too sick to travel much farther."

"We can reach Gibson City by morning," Mister Thomas said. "I know a conductor there, David Hull. He'll hide us and find a doctor to take care of Delilah. She may need to rest for several days."

Moses said, "And the rest of us? How long will it be safe for us to stay in Gibson City?"

Mister Thomas said, "It would be best to keep moving, but it's your decision whether to stay with Delilah or leave her behind."

He took off his coat and wrapped it around Delilah. "I won't need a coat tonight; I'll be plenty warm pumping the handcar. It's likely to snow tonight, and that will be both good and bad for us. It will be harder to move the handcars but the snow will hide us."

Even as I worried about Delilah, I found myself wondering what the snow would be like. Moses had told me it would be as cold as ice but as fluffy as cotton.

As we travelled along, I felt the cold creeping into my bones. The wool coat was thick and I no longer cared that it was rough on my skin. I wrapped it close around me and tried to hold the sleeves down over my hands. Mister Thomas told us to keep wriggling our toes so they wouldn't freeze. As I looked up at the night sky, I saw flakes of snow floating down, landing on everything. Then the snow started coming down thicker and thicker. I opened my mouth and let snowflakes fall on my tongue. The snow had no taste and melted in my mouth before I could even feel its coldness.

Soon the snow was lying heavy on the tracks and it was harder and harder to pump the handcars. I lost track of time. I wanted to sleep but there was no room to lie down.

When we reached a siding in Mansfield, Mister Thomas said, "Can you keep going? I know it's hard work with all this snow on the tracks." We thought about Delilah who was racked with fits of coughing, and we said we'd keep going.

Moses said, "Let me take another turn on the lever and see if you men can keep up with me!"

The men laughed. My pa said, "We'll try. We'll try."

The snow got deeper and deeper, the pumping harder and harder. Soon everyone was tired, even Moses. But then Mister Thomas said, "We've made it. We're just outside Gibson City. See that siding up ahead? There's a shed where you can hide while I go to get David Hull. I'll ask him to send for a doctor before we come back with a wagon."

We stopped the handcars on the siding and ran to the shed. Uncle Josiah carried Delilah. When he laid her down, I took her hand. She was hot with fever and her strength was leaving her. We listened to her cough and the rattle of her breath. Her teeth chattered.

Soon Mister Thomas was back with Mister Hull. We climbed into his wagon and found a welcome pile of blankets. Before we took any for ourselves, we heaped blankets on Delilah. The men tied branches behind the wagon, and the branches swept over our tracks, hiding the wheel ruts. We travelled a short distance to a small house where we were met by Missus Hull and two small children. We climbed to the attic and lay on the floor, all of us wearing our coats and wrapped in blankets to keep us warm. I was very tired.

As I tried to fall asleep, I heard Moses and Mister Thomas talking in low voices. Mister Thomas sounded worried. "I did not plan to stop here but Delilah is clearly in need of a doctor. There are many people in these parts who would be only too happy to see the bounty hunters catch you." Mister Thomas lowered his voice even more and whispered, "Have you heard of a man named Seth Concklin? About five years ago, he was helping runaways in a neighbouring state. They were captured and Seth was arrested when he went to help them. He was released from jail but, a few days later, he was found dead. Seth was David's cousin."

Moses was quiet for a few moments. "David is a brave man to be a conductor, knowing what happened to his cousin. Clearly, we cannot stay here for long. If the doctor says that Delilah cannot travel, we will have to leave her here while we move on to Chicago. With her light skin, Delilah can pass as white and she'll be safe."

While we waited for the doctor to come, Uncle Josiah tended to Delilah. He stayed close, wiping her forehead with a cool cloth and tucking blankets around her. He comforted her, saying, "Delilah, we're going to reach Canada. But first you must rest." Delilah looked at Uncle Josiah and gave him a faint smile. Then she started coughing again, gasping for breath.

Mister Thomas said, "The doctor will be coming soon.

Let's carry Delilah downstairs to a bedroom. Mister Hull will tell the doctor that Delilah is his niece. The rest of us will hide up here in the attic."

I was worried about Delilah and I could not fall asleep. I was worried about Moses and my family, too. Would the rest of us come down with the sickness? I felt my own forehead and was relieved that it was cool.

After a short while, the doctor came to the house and Mister Hull led him to the bedroom where Delilah lay, coughing. I heard the two men talking downstairs but I couldn't make out what they were saying. After the doctor left, Missus Hull came to the attic and invited us to warm ourselves around the wood stove in the kitchen. Mister Hull looked worried.

"The doctor said that Delilah has pneumonia," he said. "She is not strong enough to travel. But, with her white skin, she is safe staying in our home. I told the doctor that she is my niece from St. Louis."

Moses asked, "Was he suspicious?"

"No, I don't think so. My wife and I will care for Delilah until she's well. I don't think it's safe for the rest of you to stay here in Gibson City. You should move on. When Delilah has recovered her strength, I will take her to Chicago to rejoin you."

Uncle Josiah said, "I want to stay and care for Delilah. I don't want to leave her."

Moses took his hand in hers. "Josiah, I know you want to stay with her. But these parts are not safe for runaways. If you stay here, you could bring harm to Delilah and the Hull family, as well as yourself. This is not the way I planned for things to go. But sometimes on the Railroad, a conductor has to make a hard choice."

Uncle Josiah began to weep and Moses held him tight. We all knew then that he had fallen in love with Delilah.

CHAPTER FOURTEEN

Waiting in Chicago

WE SAID GOODBYE to Delilah and promised that we would wait for her in Chicago. Uncle Josiah wept. We wished we could stay together, but we couldn't risk being spotted in Gibson City, a small town where neighbours watched each other's comings and goings. Mister Hull drove us back to the shed where the handcars were hidden. As we thanked him, he said, "I will see you when I bring Delilah to Chicago. I wish you Godspeed."

Snow kept falling, making high drifts on the ground. Mister Thomas said we would be safe travelling by day in the midst of the snowstorm. After a train with a snow plow passed by, we would follow on the handcars, not too close, but not too far back. We would have to work hard to keep pace with the train.

We had been waiting in the shed only a short time when we heard a loud whistle. The ground shook and I was frightened. Mister Thomas opened the door a crack so we could look out. A big black steam engine was coming down the track, its plow pushing the snow aside and making two long furrows on either side of the rails.

Mister Thomas shouted, "Time to move!"

Moses and the men started pumping the handcars. Sparks flew up from the engine's smoke stack and reminded me of the sparks that had risen from the steamboat. The snow kept falling and we kept moving. After a while, the train seemed to go faster or, maybe we were slowing down as Moses and the men were getting tired. Mister Thomas said, "The snowstorm seems to be ending so we'll have to go back to travelling at night. We're coming to Paducah Junction and we'll stop there. When the sun sets, we'll get back on the cars. We should be able to reach Joliet by daybreak tomorrow."

Moses looked at Mister Thomas. "What is the plan after we reach Joliet?"

Mister Thomas said, "You have three choices. You could take the handcars to Chicago, but the spur line ends in Joliet so you'd have to go on the main track. Or you could ride the Chicago and Alton Railroad as regular passengers with forged papers saying you are freed slaves. You'd have to hope bounty hunters wouldn't look too closely at the papers. The third choice is to get the Reverend Deacon Cushing to drive you to Chicago in a wagon."

Moses laughed. "I think we have only one choice, not three. We'll go with the Reverend Deacon Cushing. These handcars have served us well and I don't want to complain, but my arms are pretty sore. As for riding the Chicago and Alton Railroad, I'm afraid the bounty hunters could be riding that train, too."

She explained to my family and me, "The Reverend Deacon Cushing is a minister who was arrested and put in jail for helping runaways. The laws of the United States say that a man can't be kept in jail for too long without a trial. The county lawyer wanted the Reverend to spend the rest of his life in jail, but that lawyer was lazy and he took a long time preparing for the case. So much time went by that the judge had to set the Reverend free."

We set off again and my ma and I took a short spell pumping the levers. I welcomed the chance to work because it made me warm, but my arms soon ached, and I was grateful when Mister Thomas took the lever again.

The snow had stopped and the clear, cold sky was filled with stars. The North Star looked closer and brighter than ever before; it gave me hope. Through the cold night, I whispered to myself, "I hope my courage will last from midnight to dawn, from slavery to freedom."

At daybreak, we pulled onto a siding outside the town of Joliet and hid in a shed while Mister Thomas went to find the Reverend Deacon Cushing. Soon I heard voices. We opened the door, looked out and saw Mister Thomas and another man. Two brown horses pulled a wagon. The horses snorted and pawed the snow on the ground.

Mister Thomas said, "This is the Reverend Deacon Cushing."

The reverend was a short, round man with a long white beard. He said, "I'll be your conductor from here to Chicago. I've put food and blankets there for you, but you'll have to hide under the canvas. I'll drive you to Chicago, to the home of Philo Carpenter."

Before we set off, Mister Thomas said, "It's time for me to say goodbye. I am needed back in Alton. I suspect there has been trouble because the bounty hunters failed to catch you." He turned to Uncle Josiah. "I know it is difficult for you to be separated from Delilah. I pray it will not be long before she joins you in Chicago."

I asked Mister Thomas whether he would take a hand-car all the way home. He laughed. "No, this time I will ride on a passenger train. As a freed slave, I have papers saying I'm not a runaway. I'm glad because Moses isn't the only one with sore arms!"

He shook hands with all of us, and my pa said, "Mister Thomas, we will never forget your kindness."

Mister Thomas answered, "And I will never forget your courage. Rebecca, your father told me you were the first to decide to run away, to live in freedom. Little will-o'-the-wisp that you are, your conviction has sustained you and your family, and I believe you will become an inspiration to others, both black and white."

My eyes filled with tears and I felt very proud. As I climbed into the back of the wagon, I wrapped myself in a blanket, but it was the words Mister Thomas had spoken that gave me warmth. I had been bone-tired for days and days, and now I just wanted to sleep.

I slept until the wagon stopped. Then I lifted a corner of the canvas and peeked out. In the broad daylight, I saw a street filled with horse-drawn wagons and people. The street was lined with stores. A bell rang, and people looked up at the steeple of a tall white church.

The Reverend Deacon Cushing came to the back of the wagon and whispered, "This is Chicago. Stay hidden until we get to Philo Carpenter's house."

The next time we stopped, the Reverend told us it was safe to come down from the wagon. He led us to a narrow, three-storey house surrounded by a white picket fence. Mister Carpenter opened the gate and welcomed us. He had white hair, like the Reverend Deacon Cushing, but instead of a beard, he had bushy white sideburns. He said, "Welcome. My name is Philo. My wife Ann and I welcome you."

Mister Carpenter led us upstairs to the third floor and showed us a row of beds. There was a small bed, a bed just for me. Tonight I would not hide in the woods, I would not hide in the back of a wagon or sleep on the floor of an attic—I would sleep on a bed! I lay down and pulled the clean blankets over me, falling asleep almost at once and sleeping for what must have been a long time. When I woke up, I looked for the Reverend. "Moses, where is the Reverend?" I asked. "I didn't thank him or say goodbye."

Moses answered, "He had to return home but he gave us his blessing."

Missus Carpenter asked us to come downstairs. On the second floor, we passed so many bedrooms I couldn't count them. Then we walked down a wide staircase with a carved banister to the main floor. Missus Carpenter led us to the dining room where white lace curtains framed the windows and a crystal chandelier hung from the ceiling. The table and chairs were made of dark polished wood, and silver trays and bowls sat on the sideboards. The walls were lined with portraits of men and women in black suits and plain dresses. I saw the table set with seven places and knew we were being invited to eat all together with these white folks. When Missus Carpenter saw the surprise on my face, she said, "There are no slaves in this house. You are our guests."

This was not the first time I had shared food with white people. We had shared meals with other conductors, but this time felt different. The dining room was beautiful. Mister and Missus Carpenter asked us questions and listened carefully to what we said. Who would have imagined that the slave girl Rebecca would be welcomed into a big house, seated at a fancy table with fine china dishes, and invited to talk with white people about the end of slavery?

Mister Carpenter said he was confident that slavery would end soon. "But I am afraid there will be a civil war between North and South before that happens. Blacks and whites together will fight for freedom, others will fight for slavery, and brother will fight brother."

I could not understand how brother could fight brother. I thought of my pa and my uncle, and I was sure they would never fight one another. What about Grower Brown and Master Jeff? Would they fight abolitionists like Mister Pickering, Mister Thomas, Mister Hull, the Reverend Deacon Cushing, Mister Carpenter and all the others?

I asked, "What will happen if the abolitionists win? Will all slaves be free?"

"Yes, when emancipation is declared, slavery will end in the South." Mister Carpenter picked up a newspaper. "There is an article here about emancipation. It foretells a difficult period for slaves after they are freed, for they have not had the opportunity to go to school or learn trades. And they have always lived under the yoke of their owners. Tell me, Rebecca, do you know how to read and write?"

I was embarrassed as I shook my head no.

"Of course not," he said. "You have not been able to go to school. You will be staying here until Delilah joins your family. You could start to learn to read and write now. Would you like that?"

"Oh, yes," I said eagerly.

"Good," he said. "All men and women should know how to read."

My ma said quietly, "If it would be no trouble, I would like to learn to read, too."

Mister Carpenter nodded his head. "Of course, Deborah. I will ask my friend who is a teacher to come tomorrow afternoon. Frances Barrier is a member of my Unitarian Church and she teaches grown-ups, as well as children."

CHAPTER FIFTEEN

Learning to Read

WAITING FOR DELILAH was difficult. Because they had so little to do, my pa and Uncle Josiah were restless, but my ma and I kept busy. In the mornings, we worked with Missus Carpenter and helped with the cooking, cleaning and laundry. In the afternoons, Mister Carpenter kept his word and Missus Barrier came to teach my ma and me how to read and write.

The teacher was a light-skinned black woman who dressed in fine clothes and wore a bonnet with pretty ribbons. Mister Carpenter introduced us. "Deborah and

Rebecca, this is my friend Frances Barrier. Some years ago she taught herself to read, and since then she has taught many grown-ups and even more children. She will teach you to read, too." When he left the room, I looked at my feet, not knowing what to say.

Missus Barrier said, "Deborah and Rebecca, when I was young I was not allowed to go to school, but I was lucky to have a friend who gave me books. I started with a primer, a simple book with one word for each picture. I studied the words and matched them to the pictures, saying the words out loud. I learned the alphabet, sounding out each letter, and soon I was reading. Here, let me show you what I mean."

Missus Barrier laid some books on a table. We stood beside her and watched as she pointed to a picture, then a word, then back to the picture. Then she asked us to try. My ma took some encouragement, but I could do it easily. I was eager to learn the alphabet, too. What would it be like to open a book and understand all the words written inside? I asked Missus Barrier, "Are the letters and words the same for white people and black people?"

She laughed, "Yes, Rebecca, they're the same for all of us. When you learn to read, it doesn't matter what colour your skin is. Your mind will be free to imagine anything you wish, to fly up into the clouds or travel around the world. I think you'll love being able to read. It'll be harder for you, Deborah, because you're older, but you'll learn. Don't worry."

Missus Barrier came every afternoon, and in the evening, I practised words, over and over. I printed out the letters and traced them. I closed my eyes, trying to remember their shape. One day I asked Missus Barrier to show me the letters in my name.

She printed out the letters of my name, "REBECCA." That night I wrote my name in a small book Missus Carpenter gave me. I was proud as I traced the letters carefully and said my name out loud. Someday I would write a letter to Miss Clarissa and tell her everything that had happened since I ran away from the plantation.

My ma struggled with the letters but she learned to write my name, then her own name, then my pa's. She said she wanted to write our names all together because we were a family; we had stayed together, even though we were slaves, then runaways. On a page of my book, she printed "OBADIAH, REBECCA, DEBORAH."

I liked living at the Carpenters' house and having Missus Barrier teach me to read. Part of me wished we could stay in Chicago, but I knew we would leave as soon as Delilah joined us. Uncle Josiah was especially anxious to see her, and Moses and my pa were anxious to keep moving. My ma was quiet. She was weary of travelling from place to place.

One night, as we sat together, Uncle Josiah told us that he and Delilah loved one another, and when she joined us in Chicago, they would be married. He would stay with her, no matter where she wanted to live—Freedom Village or Chicago or any other place.

My pa said he was happy for Uncle Josiah. "But, Brother," he said, "you and I have been apart for most of our lives. Since we came together on the Underground Railroad, we've shared danger and worry. We've shared hope, too. I don't want to be apart again. Besides, Josiah, it would be dangerous for you to settle anywhere in the United States, especially if you marry a quadroon."

Uncle Josiah laughed bitterly. "Poor Delilah, white people think she's too black to be white. And black people think she's too white to be black. Delilah has no place, but we love one another and we will make ourselves a home, a place where she belongs. I don't want to be apart from you, my brother, but I love Delilah and I will live wherever she chooses."

A few days later, Mister Carpenter received a telegram from David Hull. He and Delilah would arrive in Chi-

cago within a few days. We were excited and kept ourselves busy by working in the kitchen, making food to
celebrate their coming.

Finally, one afternoon a wagon stopped at the gate.
We looked out the window and saw Mister Hull lifting
Delilah out of the carriage. She was too weak to stand.
When they came into the house, Uncle Josiah took her
in his arms and gently carried her upstairs. Mister Hull
shook his head. "Perhaps we should have waited longer
but she insisted on joining you."

We went upstairs and found Uncle Josiah sitting beside Delilah, holding her hand. She turned her head and
smiled at us, then lay back on the pillow, weak from the
journey. Mister Carpenter sent for a doctor and, after
examining her, he said she had been foolish to travel in
her condition. She would recover only if she rested for
several weeks.

Later that night I heard Moses and Mister Carpenter
talking downstairs. Mister Carpenter said, "I am sorry to
give you bad news even as we welcome Delilah's arrival.
Word among the abolitionists is that the federal marshals are looking for you here in Chicago. Tomorrow
night they plan to start searching the homes of abolitionists, and this house will certainly be searched."

Moses said, "Delilah has to stay here and rest. She can

pass as white and she'll be safe, but the rest of us must move on. Josiah will want to stay with Delilah but I'll try to persuade him to come with us."

"Love is a powerful force," Mister Carpenter said. "As strong as you are, I doubt you will be able to persuade Josiah to leave Delilah. If need be, I will find a safe place for him to hide here in Chicago."

Moses said, "Whatever Josiah decides, the rest of us must leave Chicago tonight. The Underground Railroad usually runs from here to the border at Niagara Falls, but I fear there will be too many federal marshals and bounty hunters watching that border. I hope you can arrange another route."

Mister Carpenter said, "Yes, I have thought about that. I can arrange your passage from here to Albany, New York, on the New York Central Railroad. You won't have to pump handcars. My cousin Theodore works on the railroad, tending the caboose. He can hide you in the caboose until you reach Albany. From there, another conductor can drive you straight north to Canada."

Moses said, "What is the word about federal marshals and bounty hunters at the Albany station?"

"The situation is not good," Mister Carpenter said. "Theodore has reported that there are a large number of bounty hunters and federal marshals on the route. Let's hope that they will not see you at the Albany station. You may have to take that risk."

"Mister Carpenter," Moses said sharply, "I'm not taking these people on that railroad unless you have a better plan. I need to keep these people safe."

Mister Carpenter paused. "Instead of Albany, you could get off the train at a fueling stop in Hyde Park, north of Poughkeepsie. The train stops there for fresh water and coal; there's no station and it is most unlikely that it will be watched. I have a Quaker friend, Charles Coffin, who could meet you there."

Moses smiled. "I like that plan. Hyde Park will be just fine."

That night Moses said, "Rebecca, were you surprised by the way I talked to Mister Carpenter? When I was a slave, I had no voice. But on the Underground Railroad, I have the final say on what route we take—no one else. When I act equal to whites, I am equal. Don't you ever forget that." I vowed I would never forget what Moses said.

Moses told my pa and ma, "We're moving on tonight. Mister Carpenter will drive us to a small town in Indiana where his cousin Theodore will meet us. Now, I need to talk to Josiah."

Later on that evening Moses told us what happened,

how she knocked on the door to Delilah's room and found Uncle Josiah sitting beside her bed. Moses gently told him that he couldn't stay at the Carpenters' house because federal marshals would be searching it that very night. Uncle Josiah looked determined as he said, "I will not leave Delilah behind."

Moses nodded. "That's what I thought you would say. But the federal marshals are coming to this house tonight and, if you're here, you will be caught. You're not light-skinned like Delilah and you can't pass as white. Mister Carpenter has asked a friend of Missus Barrier to hide you. She's a widow who believes slavery is wrong but she isn't known as an abolitionist. Her house won't be searched, and you'll be safe until Delilah is well."

Uncle Josiah sighed, "I understand."

After that was settled, Moses came out of Delilah's room and said we were ready to move on. Mister Carpenter went to the window to see if there were federal marshals on the street outside. The street was empty. We hugged Uncle Josiah and Delilah and said goodbye. Tears ran down my face. We had just been united as a family and now we were being torn apart. Mister Carpenter brought his carriage to the gate, and, seeing no one, motioned for us to run from the house and climb in.

I ran as fast as I could but my legs were weak. I found it hard to swallow. At first, I thought my throat hurt from crying as we said goodbye, but once I was in the carriage my arms and legs started to ache. I didn't want to tell my pa or my ma. When Delilah became sick, she had to stay behind. I was determined not to be left in Chicago.

CHAPTER SIXTEEN

The New York Central Railroad

❧

AS WE TRAVELLED through the night, I slept in fits and starts. I awoke and felt hot, then awoke and felt cold. At last we came to a long passenger train pulled up at a siding. Workers hurried from car to car, carrying lanterns to light their way, while others shovelled coal into the coal car and filled the water tanks.

Mister Carpenter opened the carriage door. "This is a work yard. There are no bounty hunters here. The train will be underway soon and it will take you to Hyde Park.

Please follow me to the caboose, where my cousin Theodore is waiting for you."

Theodore, wearing black-and-white striped overalls and a hat of the same cloth, welcomed us and helped us climb up a ladder into the caboose. "Come in and make yourselves comfortable," he said. Mister Carpenter stood awkwardly in the middle of the crowded caboose. He promised to watch over Delilah until she and Uncle Josiah could travel to Canada. We thanked him for his kindness and he wished us Godspeed.

The train whistle sounded and Mister Carpenter quickly climbed down from the caboose. We waved farewell. Theodore scooped coal into a small stove and boiled a kettle of water. "I'll make coffee and we can have some bread and jam," he said.

I put my head on my ma's lap and let my body rock back and forth with the motion of the train. I was finally riding on a real railroad but I felt too sick to be excited. When we came to a crossing, a whistle sounded, the train slowed down and the engineer rang a bell. Then the train picked up speed and rushed on. I fell asleep and awoke only when the sun was high in the sky. When I sat up and looked out the window, I saw the reflection of my own face. At first, I did not recognize myself. I no longer looked like the slave girl from Grower Brown's plantation. I was still afraid, I was not free, and I had no home, but there was hope in my eyes. I thought of Miss Clarissa. Would she recognize me? I knew she could not even imagine all the places I had been, or all the people I had met, since I ran away from the plantation. I thought of what Mister Carpenter had said about the end of slavery. If slaves were set free in the South, what would happen to the plantation? Would I someday be able to visit Miss Clarissa without risking my freedom?

We passed small farms, villages and fields all covered in clean, white snow. Moses asked, "What are you thinking, Rebecca?" I told her I was thinking about being a conductor on the Underground Railroad, just like her. She frowned. "Child, this isn't the life for you. You'll go to school and learn to read and write like an educated person. You can help slaves more by writing than by taking them on the Railroad. And when slavery has ended, you can teach them how to read and write. They'll need people like you who've found their way."

"What do you mean?" I asked.

"You're a bright girl and you'll learn to live as a free woman. But many slaves won't have taken the journey you have taken. You can lead them."

"Mister Carpenter believes there will be a war to end slavery," I said. "Do you believe that, too?"

Moses looked at me sadly. "Yes, Rebecca, I'm afraid Mister Carpenter is right about that. There will be war. And that war will never really end if the North wins, because many people in the South won't accept that slaves should be free. People like Grower Brown, Master Jeff and the others in the Knights of the Golden Circle, they'll strike fear in the hearts of black people for many years to come." Her face looked tired and sad, and she turned to the window.

Then she turned back to me and smiled. "Maybe in Canada you'll find a nice man to marry. What do you think about that?"

I laughed. "I just want to live with my pa and ma." I looked at her and asked, "Did you ever want to marry a man?"

Moses looked surprised. "Didn't I ever tell you that I was married? Yes, Rebecca, I was married once but no more. I loved my husband and he loved me, but when I decided to be part of the Underground Railroad, he wanted to stay behind. When we met up again, years later, he had another wife—and children, too. I was mad at him, but then I figured it wasn't his fault; I was the one who left him. Sometimes I feel lonely but mostly I don't think about myself. I have many more slaves to lead to freedom."

I felt sad for her. I hoped that she would find another man to love her.

The train started to slow down and Theodore said, "We're about to arrive in Albany. I'll go inside the station to see how many bounty hunters and federal marshals there are. Sit back from the windows so you can't be seen."

We pushed our backs against the walls of the caboose, and Moses asked, "Theodore, do the federal marshals ever come aboard the trains?"

Theodore said, "Rarely, very rarely." He stepped down from the caboose, locking the door behind him. I began to feel weary and cold, even though a fire burned in the stove, and I had to lay my head on my ma's lap again.

When Theodore returned, he looked worried. "Moses, there are federal marshals checking every black passenger who gets on or off the train. And there are many bounty hunters in the station."

Moses nodded. "Then it's good we're going on to Hyde Park." She pulled her revolver out of her belt and made sure there was a bullet in every chamber. She turned to me and said, "It's for times like this that I carry a gun. But don't worry, child, I'll get you to Canada."

When the train started moving again, the sun was setting, spreading bands of orange and purple across the sky. Theodore gave us more bread and jam but my throat hurt and I couldn't swallow. My ma thought I was sick from the rocking of the train, but I knew I had a fever.

The fever made my dreams seem real. I dreamt that the train was a ship carrying us across the sea and I dreamt that I was trapped in the burning steamboat. My mouth was dry and I could barely talk. I nudged my ma and pointed to a jug of water. My ma looked at me and frowned. When she put her hand on my head, there was fear in her eyes. She said, "Obadiah, our girl is sick. Feel her head."

Pa put his rough, calloused hand gently on my forehead. His hand felt cool to me. "Oh, baby," he said, looking frightened. "Deborah, we need to get our girl to a doctor."

Theodore said, "There's a doctor in Poughkeepsie who is an abolitionist. He'll take good care of her. Hyde Park is just up the river from Poughkeepsie."

Moses tore a strip of cloth from the hem of her dress and dipped it in the bucket of water. She bathed my forehead, trying to cool me down. I slept and awoke, over and over.

Finally we reached Hyde Park. Theodore jumped from the caboose and helped the rest of us down. My pa had to carry me as we followed Theodore up a steep hill. I wondered what we would find when we got to the top.

CHAPTER SEVENTEEN

The Secret Passage

WHEN I AWOKE, I found myself on a small bed in a dark room. I couldn't remember how I got there. A doctor stood over me and said, "Rebecca, you have scarlet fever. You need to rest."

A small white woman in a plain black dress stood beside my bed. She asked, "How long will it be before she is strong again?"

The doctor said, "At least a month, maybe longer." He picked up his black leather bag. "Keep the curtains drawn so the light doesn't hurt her eyes. I'll be back tomorrow."

My ma sat beside my bed while Moses and my pa sat on a blanket on the floor. The darkened room was crowded. The white woman smiled at me and said, "Rebecca, my name is Lucretia Mott. My brother, Charles Coffin, lives here and I am visiting. I visit him as often as possible for, when he is alone, my brother neglects to eat properly and the house is never tidied."

She paused. "I'm sorry, Rebecca. I shouldn't be talking so much. I just want you to know that you are safe here and I will stay to help nurse you. I will write to my husband and tell him I must stay here. I'm sure he will understand."

"Where am I?" I asked.

"You arrived last night. You rode in a caboose to Hyde Park, do you remember that? Then my brother brought you here, to his house in Poughkeepsie. Now you're in a hidden room and you are safe. You can reach this room only by stairs that run through a secret passage, and the door to the stairs is hidden in the pantry. Many runaways have hidden here, and no federal marshal has ever found the passage."

During the day we all stayed in the hidden room and Missus Mott brought us food and water, but at night, Moses and my pa went downstairs while my ma stayed with me. I slept and sometimes I couldn't tell whether I was awake or dreaming.

One night, I heard Moses say, "It's very risky for us to stay in one place for a month."

Mister Coffin answered, "Moses, I'm afraid I agree. Rebecca must remain here, of course, until she's well. And Deborah, because the child needs her mother. But you and Obadiah should move to a different house. Perhaps you should even go ahead to Canada? The southerners are putting great pressure on the federal marshals to enforce the Fugitive Slave Act. They are threatening to leave the Union of the United States if the law is not enforced. They are insisting that the federal marshals capture and return runaways. My brother is a judge at the courthouse here in Poughkeepsie. The federal marshals have an office there, as well, and he has heard them talking. They are determined to arrest you, Moses."

"Does your brother know we're here? Will he be able to give warning if the federal marshals come for us?" Moses asked.

Mister Coffin chose his words carefully. "My brother has taken an oath of loyalty to the federal government and he feels beholden to that oath, although he believes that slavery must end. He has promised me, that if he hears that the federal marshals are coming to search this house, he will come to the front door wearing a white hat. That will be the sign."

When I heard Mister Coffin ask whether my pa and Moses should go ahead to Canada, I could not stop the tears from running down my face. My ma got up from the floor, sat on the edge of my bed and wrapped her arms around me. "Don't worry, Rebecca. Your pa may have to stay at a different house, but he will not leave you behind."

Mister Coffin arranged for Moses and my pa to move to another house in Poughkeepsie. My ma and I cried as we said goodbye, but it was a comfort to know that they would be nearby.

I was getting stronger, and, one evening, Missus Mott helped me walk to a sitting room on the second floor. She lit a fire in a brick fireplace and made tea in an iron kettle. She saw me looking at the books that lined the room and asked me whether I knew how to read. When I told her I had started to learn to read at the Carpenters' house in Chicago, she went to the shelves and pulled out a heavy book covered with green leather. Together, we looked at prints of birds and flowers.

I tried to read the words printed below the pictures

but they were too hard. Missus Mott laughed, "Those words are in Latin. It's no wonder they're hard for you to read." She promised to find a primer for me. She said, "No person, man or woman, black or white, should lack an understanding of the written word. Words are important in the battle against slavery."

The next day, Missus Mott brought a slate tablet and a copy of *The New England Primer* to the sitting room. She traced the letters of the alphabet on the tablet and asked me to say each letter's name. I was pleased that I remembered most of them. She opened the book, a book with pictures and simple words, and soon I was able to read them. My ma joined us and worked hard to learn the alphabet. She confused some letters but she was learning.

One day Missus Mott suggested that, after I learned to read, I could write down our story, the story of our journey to freedom. I thought of all the brave people who had helped us, and I was pleased to think I could write their names in a book and tell the story of our flight from slavery.

Missus Mott said, "In the meantime, do you want to write a letter to your father?" I missed my pa and I missed Moses, too. I had not seen them for almost a month. My ma asked Missus Mott if she would help her write a letter to my pa, too. My pa could not read but the family who were hiding him would read the letters for him. I told Missus Mott I might want to be a teacher when I grew up so I could teach my pa how to read.

One night at dinner, Mister Coffin read an article from an abolitionist newspaper, an article about Buxton, a settlement in Upper Canada. The article was written about Reverend William King, a Presbyterian minister and abolitionist. When his father-in-law died, he was dismayed to learn that he had inherited a number of slaves as well as a plantation in Louisiana.

He sold the plantation and brought all of the slaves to Canada so they could live in freedom. He bought a large tract of land—9,000 acres—in Upper Canada and founded an agricultural settlement. He arranged for a school to be built and hired a teacher. Mister Coffin suggested that we might want to settle in Buxton, a place where we would be welcomed. He said, "In that settlement, Obadiah could buy land to farm at $2.50 per acre, on credit, and Rebecca could attend a good school."

My ma thanked Mister Coffin. "I will tell Obadiah about this. I am still surprised to learn of the goodness of so many people, like this Reverend King. Until I started riding the Underground Railroad, I didn't know that there were so many good people, both black and white."

One day I asked Missus Mott to tell me about her life. She told me that some years ago, a friend named Elizabeth Cady Stanton invited Missus Mott to go with her to the World Anti-Slavery Convention in London, England. Missus Mott said, "She changed my life forever. I was an abolitionist but, after that trip, I was also a suffragette. I realized that women in the United States and many other countries are not really free. Under the law, I cannot own property and I cannot vote. I don't have a voice in choosing our president or our governor or any other elected official. I'm fortunate to have a loving husband and two kind brothers, but I would like to be equal to them under the law. Equality for women is something to fight for—just like freedom from slavery."

I asked, "Are there suffragettes in Canada?"

Missus Mott laughed, "Yes. Maybe you will have to be both a suffragette and an abolitionist."

That night I heard Mister Coffin talking to his sister. He said, "I'm worried, Lucretia. The courthouse is crowded with federal marshals."

Missus Mott said, "The doctor is pleased with Rebecca's progress. If Deborah and Rebecca need to leave now, the child is strong enough. I will miss her very much."

"Yes," Mister Coffin said, "I will miss her, too, and the house will be very quiet. It is a great sorrow to me that I have no children, but God has given me a blessing by calling me to shelter runaways."

The next day, I heard a knock at the front door. I looked out the second-floor window while Missus Mott went downstairs. I saw a man standing at the door, a man in a white hat, and I knew what that meant. The federal marshals were coming.

Mister Coffin sent word to Moses and my pa to be ready to flee with us. He said, "Deborah, please gather warm clothes and blankets. I'll get the carriage ready and bring it to the back lane. We'll pick up Moses and Obadiah on the way north."

Missus Mott packed food for us. I tore a page from the small book Missus Carpenter had given me. I wrote, "My name is Rebecca. I am going to Canada and I will be free." I left the paper in the hidden room at the top of the secret passage and hoped other runaways would find it when they stopped at this house.

CHAPTER EIGHTEEN

Dawn in Canada

BEFORE WE SET OFF from Mister Coffin's house, we heard a rider approaching from the main road. He was breathless from the ride. "I was too late," he moaned. "When I got to the house where Moses and Obadiah had been hiding, the federal marshals had surrounded it. They led Moses and Obadiah out of the house in handcuffs and took them to the county jail." The rider looked at me and my ma. "I'm very sorry to bring such terrible news."

Mister Coffin put his hand on the man's shoulder.

"You did your best. It is no fault of yours that they were captured." At the thought of my pa and Moses in jail, I started to cry and could not stop. We had come so far and it seemed cruel that they had been captured so close to Canada. Mister Coffin tried to comfort me. "Don't worry, Rebecca. God will help us find a way to get your father and Moses out of that jail." My ma hugged me and I held tight to her. Our tears ran together.

Mister Coffin said, "We have to make sure you two are safe while we figure out how to free Moses and your father." To our surprise, Mister Coffin took us to the house where Moses and my pa had been hidden. He explained, "The federal marshals have already searched here, and they won't come back any time soon." We were led to another secret room. I imagined my pa and Moses spending days in that same room, waiting for me to be well. If only I had not gotten sick!

That night Mister Coffin gathered hundreds of people from all the churches in Poughkeepsie—white and black. They met at the Friends' Meeting House and Mister Coffin asked them to spread the word that two runaways needed their help. "Spread the word in your congregations; tell the people to come to the Dutchess County courthouse at ten o'clock tomorrow morning. Harriet Tubman, the woman called Moses, and a good man named Obadiah will be arraigned then. They seek freedom, and we must see to it that they are not sent back to the bondage of slavery."

In the morning, throngs of people drove their wagons to Market Street. At ten o'clock, every church bell in Poughkeepsie started ringing and people marched to the courthouse. As Moses and my pa were led up the steps, people moved forward, making a circle that tightened around the federal marshals and the prisoners. The marshals struggled to stay on their feet, and I lost sight of my pa and Moses as they were swept into the crowd.

People ran in all directions. The door to our carriage was flung open, and my pa and Moses were lifted onto a seat. They were free! Then all the wagons drove off in different directions. There were not enough federal marshals to follow all the wagons and they had to guess which one was carrying Moses and my pa. Luckily, they guessed wrong, and no one followed us.

My pa and Moses hugged my ma and me. Moses laughed, "Well, we are bound for freedom again! Those fine people in Poughkeepsie sure did surprise the federal marshals."

My pa said, "They surprised me, too! At first I was scared when I saw all those people coming to the courthouse. I was afraid they were a mob, but when I looked out, I saw many black faces and people dressed like Quakers. I looked at Moses and she was grinning from ear to ear. I knew then that those people were going to save us."

Moses decided that we should drive straight north towards Canada. Mister Coffin drove day and night, stopping at the homes of Friends and other abolitionists to harness fresh horses. Snow fell and the horses struggled to run through the deepening drifts. Would we be forced to stop?

After several days, Mister Coffin drove to a farmhouse. He was tired, his face lined with weariness. A Friend welcomed us and offered us a wooden sleigh with metal runners. Mister Coffin harnessed the horses to the traces on the sleigh and we were off. The sleigh flew down narrow roads, across fields, and through thick forests. The snow kept falling, hiding us in its swirling whiteness. We were invisible and I felt safe again.

Moses pointed to a tree. "Look, see that sign up ahead? I can't read it but I know when we pass by it, we will be free! We will be in Canada!" We were silent as we crossed that border, a border marked only by a faded wooden sign. We looked at one another, hardly believing that we were truly beyond the reach of slavery. I felt a deep joy and my eyes filled with tears. Our worry and fear lifted from our shoulders. I remembered a passage from the Bible that talked about rebirth. At that moment, I felt I had been reborn. We were no longer slaves or runaways. We were free people, starting new lives in a new land.

The sleigh went on through the snow-covered forest until we reached a log house on the edge of a small town. A young couple, Bernard and Maria, welcomed us and said we must celebrate our freedom together. Maria fed us thick soup and fresh bread while Bernard made beds for us on the floor near a stone fireplace. They spoke French to one another but English to us. I struggled to understand their words, but it was not hard to understand the warmth of their welcome.

After resting for a few days, Mister Coffin said it was time for him to return to Poughkeepsie. I asked him to thank Missus Mott, and I promised to write and tell her about our life in Canada. Mister Coffin told us that Bernard and Maria would help us whether we stayed in Lower Canada or continued on to Upper Canada. My pa said we wanted to go to Buxton in Upper Canada, to the settlement Reverend King had founded. Mister Coffin nodded. "I think you will have a good life there and you will be welcomed by neighbours who have also travelled from slavery to freedom. I wish you every blessing. It has been an honour to help you."

Moses walked Mister Coffin to the door and sniffed the clear, cold air. "I'm glad to be in Canada, the only place where I feel truly safe, safe from the harsh laws of America. I'll stay here a while before I go back to the South, but not too long. There are other slaves waiting to ride the Underground Railroad."

We waved goodbye to Mister Coffin and wished him Godspeed on his return journey. I had reached freedom with the help of freed slaves, Quakers, Unitarians, Presbyterians, Methodists and other abolitionists, all of them committed to the belief that slavery should end. Now my parents and I—we were free. The good people on the Underground Railroad had helped me to freedom, but they had laid a weight on my shoulders, too, and I knew that, all my life, I would fight for justice for all people, black and white.

That night, Maria gently shook me awake. She led me to the window and we looked out at a sky ablaze with colour. "*C'est l'aurore boréale* . . . it is the northern lights," she said. Veils of light danced in the sky, swirling above the horizon. Green, blue, orange, yellow. In Canada, there was light even before the dawn.

LATER EVENTS IN
THE FIGHT FOR EQUALITY

■ Moses (Harriet Tubman) was never caught. She rescued hundreds of slaves. During the Civil War, she worked as a scout for the Union Army of the North. After the Civil War, she stayed in America and settled in Auburn, New York. She was married, for the second time, to a kind and gentle man. When slavery ended, she fought for the rights of women. She died in 1913 at the age of ninety-one.

■ In 1861, the Civil War began in the United States. The war was fought between the North and the South. The North wanted to end slavery; the South wanted to preserve it. Brother fought brother, just as Mister Carpenter foretold.

■ When the Emancipation Proclamation was passed by the United States Congress on the 1st of January, 1863, slaves were freed in all Confederate states. The Confederate Army surrendered on the 9th of April, 1865, and the Civil War officially ended.

■ Former members of the Knights of the Golden Circle joined new secret armies such as the Klu Klux Klan and the Red Shirts. Their goal was to preserve a society based on the subjugation of black people.

■ On the 14th of April, 1865, John Wilkes Booth assassinated President Abraham Lincoln at Ford's Theatre in Washington, D.C. John Wilkes Booth was alleged to be a Knight of the Golden Circle.

■ The Thirteenth Amendment to the United States Constitution was adopted on the 18th of December, 1865. With its passage, slavery was abolished in the United States of America forever. The Fourteenth Amendment, adopted in 1868, included the Citizenship Clause that provided an inclusive definition of citizenship, overruling the Dred Scott decision of 1857 which said that descendants of African slaves could not be citizens of the United States. The North hired teachers and built schools in the South during the Reconstruction Era. These schools educated the poor, but there were separate schools for blacks and whites.

■ In 1917, women in Ontario (formerly called Upper Canada) were granted the right to vote by provincial legislation, and in 1918, the federal government granted women over the age of 21 the right to vote. For Indigenous peoples, and for some ethnic minorities, the right to vote remained out of reach for decades to come.

■ In 1920, the Nineteenth Amendment to the U.S. Constitution granted American women the right to vote, a right known as suffrage. As was the case in Canada, restrictions and procedures based on race prevented some U.S. citizens from voting until later in the century.

■ In 1925, the Historic Sites and Monuments Board of Canada recognized the importance of the Underground Railroad. From the 1830s through the 1860s, thousands of runaways settled in Canada and established new communities dedicated to the ideals of tolerance and equality under the law. Despite incidents of prejudice, the newcomers became loyal and active citizens in communities across southwestern Ontario, as well as other areas. In 1999, a series of initiatives were carried out to further commemorate the sites and people of the Underground Railroad in Canada. In October of 2001, Parks Canada installed the Tower of Freedom monument in Windsor, Ontario.

■ On the 2nd of July, 1964, American President Lyndon Johnson signed the Civil Rights Act of 1964 to outlaw discrimination based on race, colour, religion, sex or national origin. Among other provisions, the Act ended unequal voter registration procedures and racial segregation in schools.

■ In Canada, the Constitution Act was passed in 1982 and guaranteed rights and freedoms under the law. Section 15, Equality Rights, provides for equality "before and under the law and equal protection and benefit of law . . . without discrimination based on race, national or ethnic origin, colour, religion, sex, age or mental or physical disability."

■ Around the world, the fight for equality and civil rights continues to this day.

ACKNOWLEDGEMENTS

We are deeply indebted to Ron and Veronica Hatch and the staff at Ronsdale Press for their editorial guidance. Without their insight, support and patience, this book would never have reached the public. We wish to thank our eight grandchildren—Zoe, Sacha, Eli, Anaïs, Yemaya, Alder, Ronan and Bronwen—for their abiding interest in bedtime stories. They were the first audience for *Railroad of Courage* and insisted that the story of Rebecca, a girl born into slavery, be told in the context of hope and courage against the evil of slavery.

We want to acknowledge the courage and conviction of every link in the Underground Railroad, a movement that united people of conscience in the 1800s. This book was written as a testament to the actual conductors and abolitionists who sustained the Underground Railroad: Harriet Tubman (Moses), Alexander Milton Ross (the Birdman), James P. Thomas, William Still, Priscilla Baltimore, Elijah Parish Lovejoy, David Hull, Seth Concklin, the Reverend Deacon Cushing, Philo and Ann Carpenter, and Lucretia Mott. It is unknown whether these historical figures ever met and the events in this story are fiction, as are all other characters. All references to laws of the day in Canada and America are based on historical fact.

We are indebted to Eric Foner for articulating the workings of the Underground Railroad in *Gateway to Freedom: The Hidden History of the Underground Railroad*. We acknowledge the extensive work that Historica Canada and Black History Canada have done to document the central role of Canada in the Underground Railroad. We are also indebted to many historical societies across North America, such as the Alton Historical Society, which have kept the history of the Underground Railroad alive and accessible for current generations.

During the decades when the Underground Railroad was active, Canada provided hope and a destination for thousands of runaway slaves. Without Canada, where would runaways have found freedom? We fervently hope that Canada, among other nations, will shelter those who seek freedom in our time.

Dan's interest in slavery began when he went to the Pough-keepsie Day School in New York State. The school was in an old three-storey house that had been a stop on the Underground Railroad. The Underground Railroad was a chain of freed blacks, runaway slaves and abolitionists who helped runaways to reach freedom in Canada. The Railroad was a great work of moral imagination driven by the courage of slaves and people of conscience.

Dan and his classmates spent many hours searching for a secret passage and a room where runaway slaves were hidden. They never found the secret passage but, at night, as Dan lay in bed, he thought about the Underground Railroad and wondered, "If I had been born a slave, would I have had the courage to run away?"

Nancy grew up in a small town in Illinois where she saw the residue of slavery, fear and distrust among the people around her. In 1970, the United States was again a nation divided, and people of conscience felt compelled to practise civil disobedience. Dan and Nancy moved to Canada, a more open and united country, and they decided to settle there permanently.

When their three children were little, Dan and Nancy enjoyed telling them bedtime stories. Those children grew up, as children do, and had children of their own. Now Dan and Nancy tell stories to their eight grandchildren and hope they do not grow up too soon.

For educational resources and information about their work, please visit their website at: www.rubenstein-dyson.com.

MARQUIS

Québec, Canada